"These stories pulse with the stuff of impassioned observation and level-headed confidence. Deepa Rajagopalan takes no reader for granted, and wins her glowing arrival with a beautiful, rich, savvy book. If any peacocks were harmed in its making, there isn't a feather out of place."

—Canisia Lubrin, author of *Code Noir*

"*Peacocks of Instagram* offers candid snapshots of the intimacies, the small braveries, and the strange twists of fate that shape and connect ordinary people across time and continents. At once piercing and tender, these stories are richly textured and glittering with gorgeous detail. Rajagopalan's characters are dreamers and survivors, risk-takers and rule-breakers—you'll be rooting for each and every one of them from the first page to the last. A fresh voice in Canadian storytelling and a must-read collection!"

—Anuja Varghese, author of *Chrysalis*

"Deepa Rajagopalan is a masterful storyteller. In her brilliant debut collection, *Peacocks of Instagram*, she unveils a world where powerful, ambitious Indian women redefine life on their own terms. In this exquisite symphony of belonging, she deftly challenges conventions with breathtaking prose. Get ready to be captivated by a writer poised to reshape literature."

—Chelene Knight, author of *Junie*

"Inhabiting children's and adult perspectives with equal acuity, Deepa Rajagopalan has a finely tuned, confident voice and a seemingly effortless knack for evoking pathos in the dynamics between her diverse, and often fractious, cast of characters. *Peacocks of Instagram* is a mature, honest collection of stories that thoughtfully examine themes of agency and power, a book as beautifully written as it is emotionally affecting."

—Pasha Malla, author of *Kill the Mall*

"*Peacocks of Instagram* is brimming with humour, wit, and sharp-eyed insight. These are tales about the immigrant hustle and the pain of being overlooked. They explore transgressions and betrayals between friends and lovers. Spanning countries and continents, Deepa Rajagopalan's stories show us that, in spite of it all, we can persevere. A gorgeous debut by a genuine talent."

—Sindya Bhanoo, author of *Seeking Fortune Elsewhere*

Peacocks of Instagram

STORIES

DEEPA RAJAGOPALAN

Published in Canada and the USA in 2024 by House of Anansi Press Inc.
houseofanansi.com

28 27 26 25 24   1 2 3 4 5

Library and Archives Canada Cataloguing in Publication

Title: Peacocks of Instagram : stories / Deepa Rajagopalan.
Names: Rajagopalan, Deepa, author.
Identifiers: Canadiana (print) 20230582443 | Canadiana (ebook) 2023058246X |
ISBN 9781487012403 (softcover) | ISBN 9781487012410 (EPUB)
Subjects: LCGFT: Short stories.
Classification: LCC PS8635.A454 P43 2024 | DDC C813/.6—dc23

Book design: Lucia Kim
Cover image: Master1305 @ Shutterstock

House of Anansi Press is grateful for the privilege to work on and create from the Traditional Territory of many Nations, including the Anishinabeg, the Wendat, and the Haudenosaunee, as well as the Treaty Lands of the Mississaugas of the Credit.

**Canada Council
for the Arts**

**Conseil des Arts
du Canada**

ONTARIO ARTS COUNCIL
CONSEIL DES ARTS DE L'ONTARIO
an Ontario government agency
un organisme du gouvernement de l'Ontario

With the participation of the Government of Canada
Avec la participation du gouvernement du Canada

We acknowledge for their financial support of our publishing program the Canada Council for the Arts, the Ontario Arts Council, and the Government of Canada.

Printed and bound in Canada

MIX
Paper from
responsible sources
FSC® C103567

For my Ahana.
May you always be kind, especially to yourself.

From tiny experiences we build cathedrals.
—Orhan Pamuk

Contents

Peacocks of Instagram

I MAKE A GOOD LIVING. I have a business selling peacock accessories on the internet. Earrings, bracelets, pendants, sleep masks—that sort of thing. Unlike other birds, the peacock does not derive its colours purely from pigments but from a combination of pigments and photonic crystals. This combination is what causes the feathers of the peacock to be iridescent, creating a shimmering look. The essence of a single peacock feather is this: the eye a deep royal blue, an inverted heart shape, and around it, layers of glossy turquoise, brown, yellow, and shades of green. I capture this essence in every accessory I make using beads, fabric, and sometimes, real peacock feathers. I make them by hand, and people here will pay ridiculous sums of money for anything handmade.

I also work at the coffee shop by the mall. I have worked here for seventeen years. Three owners have come and gone; the average turnover of the other employees is about six months, but I have been the rock of the establishment. The local paper even did an article about me. It was good publicity for the store. I have seen the minimum wage go from $8.92 to $14. More recently, I almost single-handedly brought up our online rating from 2.9 (burnt bagels, stale doughnuts, nineteen-minute wait at the drive-through) to 4.4 (excellent customer service, the Indian cashier lady made my day, good location, friendly staff, good variety).

Most of the other employees look at this job as an unpleasant rite of passage on the way to greater things. They put on blinders and do their bare minimums. Except for Celina and me. Celina works hard, but she gets into trouble because she is loud and speaks her mind. She was an actor back in the Philippines, but now she works here to put her son through university. A lot of the employees are students themselves, studying calculus and engineering and business. I only studied until the tenth grade back in Kerala.

I do my best—smiling brightly as customers walk in, chatting as I enter their orders, and making eye contact as I hand them their lattes. The key is to make them feel special, like you've been waiting all week to see them. Confidence is important. And you must come across as somewhat cool, not trying too hard. I learned this the hard way. No one wants to deal with an over-eager Indian woman with a thick Malayali accent. And you have to dress the part. I usually wear bright red lipstick, which complements my skin tone, and winged eyeliner. My uniform is always ironed. Most days, I wear my peacock earrings or bracelets. They are good conversation starters, and, after having worked here for so long, I can do as I please. Very often, customers want to buy my products, especially the ladies who wear cashmere sweaters and toques with pompoms. When they hear words like "handmade," "local," and "organic cotton," they get excited. And excitement is good for business.

My earliest memory of seeing a peacock was with my family at the Krishna temple back home in Kerala. The temple had a few resident peacocks and peahens. One of the birds that was sitting in the middle of the courtyard stood up, strutted toward us, and began splaying out its feathers. It was strange and magnificent, but at that age—I must have been three or four—I was afraid and hid behind my father. He picked me up and told me there was nothing to worry about. And he told me that the peacock can foretell the rains. When it danced, it meant the clouds would soon burst and water our crops. Years later, my husband would tell me that this peacock story was one of the more ignorant ones he had heard.

My husband is a peafowl researcher (if you say "peacock," he will lose it and say, "I don't just study one gender; in fact, I specialize in sexual selection"). I met Kannan in Kerala twenty years ago when he was studying peafowl at a sanctuary in Idukki. I was seventeen. After my family was cremated, I was offered a job as a live-in caregiver for a paralyzed man. I said yes immediately and left the house I had grown up in.

My family had lived in a thatched-roof mud house with a single room: the living room, kitchen, and bedroom all in the same space. The bathroom was outside, and if my sister or I needed to go in the middle of the night, it was a family affair—our mother would light the kerosene lantern, our father would step out first to make sure there weren't any snakes about, and then off we'd go to the outhouse, listening to crickets and howling dogs. Above our front door, a black and white photograph of my parents on their wedding day hung at an angle. My parents must have been in their early twenties in that picture, but they already looked tired and disillusioned with life, my mother with a sulky expression and my father angry. The only other thing on the wall was a Malayalam calendar, on which my father diligently crossed out the days as they passed, as if waiting for something to end. The floor of the house was made of compacted mud through which the roots of our peepal tree protruded like a camel's hump. When I was little, I used to sit on the bump and pretend I was an Arab sheikh riding his mount.

My employer used to work in Dubai and his family was accustomed to a certain lifestyle, which they couldn't keep up since his heart attack and subsequent paralysis. So they rented out the second floor of their six-bedroom house, which had marble floors and teak furniture. Kannan was one of their paying guests. I was worried when he started showing interest in me. He said he didn't care if he was seen with the house help, but I couldn't risk it. I didn't want people thinking I was sleeping my way out of a life in domestic work. And in the beginning I doubted his intentions, even when he said he wanted to marry me. That kind of thing rarely happened to people like me. I think Kannan liked me because he had never met a girl who wasn't turned off by the whole peafowl situation. On the contrary, I liked that he was so passionate about what he did, even when no one else cared about it. Eventually I said yes, even though he was just two years younger than my father, because I wanted to get out of Kerala. Kannan was based in Toronto, and in my imagination then, Canada was pristine, with wide open spaces and people who minded their own business, where no one knew me and no one would feel pity for me. Where I could make a fresh start. Soon after we arrived, Kannan signed me up for ESL classes, and within a year, I got this job at the coffee shop. I started at the back, buttering bagels, and worked my way up.

We never had a child. I was afraid of the permanence of having one. What if I lost my job, or Kannan left me, or our money disappeared one day? We couldn't get rid of the child. I didn't want to feel the way my parents did for most of their lives. Kannan didn't mind because he travelled a lot, and he didn't think it would be fair to leave the child-rearing responsibility all to me.

Kannan still travels a lot: to Florida, Texas, British Columbia, Madhya Pradesh. He has spent most of his life studying why evolution invested so much energy in the vibrant peacock plumage. He straps little hats with cameras on the peahens and peacocks to track their gazes during mating season. He spends hours studying these videos to understand what the peahen looks for in a suitable mate, and what the peacock looks for while sizing up a rival. Some nights, we watch peacock displays together in the living room, drinking wine. We see the peacock from the peahen's perspective. The peacock spreads out its feather train in a concave semicircle more than six feet long and then rattles it vigorously. Kannan tells me that the longer the train, the more force the peacock has to exert. The eyes of the feathers stay still like a thousand bullseyes, while the rest of the plumage—all this turquoise, green, and yellow—vibrates, and if you look long enough, you go into a trance, mesmerised by this extravagant show. And all the rattling makes a sound like waves crashing onto the shore. Kannan sometimes starts moving his body to match the vibrations of the peacock. And sometimes he gets turned on and wants to have sex.

Kannan is lucky to have this singular, steadfast obsession to fill his days and nights. Thanks to him, I know several peafowl facts, and I try to use them to my advantage. When a customer at the coffee shop compliments one of my accessories, I say something like, "Did you know that only the peacock—that is, the male of the species—has the flashy blue and green plumage?" Once I have their attention, I provide more information: "The female, or the peahen, has dull brown feathers because she needs to blend in with her surroundings to guard her eggs and chicks. But she gets to choose whom she wants to mate with. If the female isn't interested, nothing will happen. So the males have to work hard to attract her." Then I casually say, "I have a page on Instagram—Peacocks of Instagram—if you like this kind of thing." I want my customers to feel like a refreshing splash of water has awakened them from the drudgery of daily life. And by the end of the day, I have gathered a few followers, which eventually leads to some sales.

Late one morning in winter, a customer said she was strictly against hunting birds to make jewellery and I told her that peacocks are not hunted for their feathers. The peacock sheds its entire tail after mating season, like a snake sheds its skin. At that moment, a crowd walked into the café. The doors were held open by a relay of at least twenty people wielding placards, letting in a frosty draft and, with it, an air of heady excitement and fear. I squinted to read the signs, which were slowly being deposited on tables or propped against walls. I tried to piece together the words on T-shirts as people shuffled around, unzipping their thick winter coats. SAVE. SUPPORT. STAND.

Save what? Support whom? Celina and I made eye contact, and she looked as puzzled as I was. The café got quite loud, and for a moment, Angelo, our new store manager, got worried. He assumed the people were going to cause trouble, but it turned out they were simply peaceful protesters who wanted coffee and some warmth after standing out in the cold for a while.

A man wearing a North Face jacket came up to the cash and ordered a double-double. He wore a toque that read FARMERS NOT TERRORISTS, and suddenly the signs began to make sense to me. Save Farmers. Support Farmers. I poured the coffee into the cup and added two pumps of cream and two pumps of sugar syrup. The man held a handwritten sign under his arm, and Celina asked, "What does your sign say?"

He held it out for both of us to see. WE SUPPORT FARMERS IN PUNJAB, it read. He explained to Celina that the Indian government was imposing new laws that were detrimental to farmers without consulting them. He said that more than half a billion people would be affected. He turned to me and said, "It's like if workers here didn't have a minimum wage." He was looking for camaraderie from a fellow South Asian, but I simply said, "Here's your medium double-double."

The air in the store shifted. Something inside me, too. Although the protesters had become quiet, their presence was making the other customers and the employees nervous on that frigid February morning. Bad ratings are usually the result of bad moods and bad weather. Angelo was oblivious to this tendency. During such times, it's important to be calm and friendly and provide fast service. Instead, Angelo went about as usual, yelling at Celina that the croissants needed to be restocked and a cheese croissant was in the plain croissant tray. He pronounced croissant like "krwasan," and Celina muttered to me, "Who is he trying to impress?"

The man in the North Face jacket returned for more coffee before the lunchtime rush. He asked me if he could put up a poster on our notice board. Angelo was supposed to approve these things, but he deferred to me because he was new.

The poster showed a graphic of a man in an orange turban, and in big, bold, black letters, it read:

SAVE OUR FARMERS

NO FARMERS

NO FOOD

At the bottom was a link to an online campaign for donations. As I studied the poster, the man seemed to study my name tag. He said, "Kala, it is critical for us to help our farmers. The Indian government is putting their livelihoods at risk. And when they are peacefully protesting, they are being called terrorists. Imagine that—calling farmers terrorists! Police are using force against them." I noticed he wore a turban not unlike the one on the poster. "The donations will be used to bring supplies—milk, vegetables, sanitary napkins and such items—to the hundreds of thousands of people who are protesting in camps outside Delhi."

I waited for him to pause and said, "I'm sorry, dear. We're only allowed to put up posters offering free community programs."

My insides began to feel like they were on fire. It had taken years of meticulously avoiding anything that reminded me of the home I had left behind in Kerala to help me get over what had happened. I had made a point of avoiding the news from the subcontinent. I had never been back to India. These days, however, social media served up the news whether you wanted to see it or not. Ever since Rihanna tweeted about the farmers' protest in India, it was all over Instagram. Right-wing nationalists were calling her a slut for interfering in "internal" affairs, and journalists and comedians were being put behind bars for speaking out—the kind of intolerance that was becoming so commonplace these days. The internet was even temporarily shut down in parts of Delhi.

The problem with blocking out a time of your life is

that you cannot be selective: you have to give up the good with the bad. Even the mundane. The songs my father used to sing, the colour of my mother's eyes, the curl in my sister's pigtails—all the little things. Sometimes I tried to remember the words of the prayer my mother used to say when she lit the evening lamp by the sacred tulsi plant. Or the way we caught fireflies under the massive peepal tree outside our little house. But when I slept, I would inevitably end up in this nightmare: *I am standing on a stepstool under a wooden gallows. A noose slips over my head and the stepstool disappears. I am suspended in the air. I hear my father say, "Don't fight it."*

I never told Kannan what happened in my nightmare; I simply said I didn't remember it when I woke up. And he tried to figure out the cause of my disturbed sleep the way he tried to figure out everything in life—by gathering data. He kept a log of the things I did during the day to gather empirical evidence upon which to base his theories. He called me three to four times a day to gather data. An entry would look something like this:

Date: January 10
Daily Log: Drank a protein smoothie for breakfast, worked the 7 a.m. to 3 p.m. shift, ate a cinnamon raisin bagel for lunch, spent three hours on Instagram, did not go for the customary evening walk, ate rice and mango pickle at 10 p.m.

Quality of Sleep: Woke up at 2:45 a.m. shouting, "I can't breathe!" And then woke again at 4 a.m., screaming something indecipherable.

His diagnoses were mostly predictable, sometimes surprising, but always earnest. Too much protein or sodium, or too many carbs. Too little exercise. Too much social media. I agreed with his theories because I wondered how comforting it would be to look at life the way he did.

Twenty years ago now. My father was a black-pepper farmer in Kerala. Like everyone else, we were dependent on the rains. No rain, too much rain. We talked about the weather nearly every night. My father blamed the government for everything. My mother worked at the Krishna temple, washing the floors, cleaning the drains.

When my sister was born, things got worse for us. My sister suffered from recurrent pneumonia and needed a lot of care and medication. My mother couldn't work, and my father decided that I should take her job at the temple. He stopped me from going to school after the tenth grade because we couldn't afford to buy books.

That year, the monsoons were outrageous and destroyed my father's pepper vines. Over the years, he had taken on loans to pay for my sister's medical needs, and now he couldn't pay them off. The money lender's men started showing up at our house in lungis folded at the thighs, reeking of toddy, to threaten my father. He would just drop his head and beg them for more time.

My father had given up long before he gave up his life.

By the time of the farmers' protest, I hadn't thought about that day in years. Even Kannan didn't know the details. He used to tell me to go to therapy, but I told him that if a therapist heard my story, they'd quit!

Once I told him I wished I would get into a car crash and lose my memory like the characters in soap operas.

He said, "If you lost your memory, you would forget me. And I don't think I'd be able to win you over again."

When it was time for my break, I decided to go for a quick walk to clear my head. I was on my way to the back parking lot to grab my headphones from the car when I saw the man in the North Face jacket. He was parked right beside me and was loading his backpack and signs into the trunk of his car. As he packed, he told me that his family came from a Sikh farming community in Punjab.

"There is a farmer suicide epidemic in India," he said. "It's not an isolated problem. I'm not sure if you're aware of what these new farm laws mean, but essentially, they are death warrants for small and marginalized farmers. They will be left at the mercy of corporations. I'm just trying to raise awareness, do my part." He paused and then added, "We all should."

I had the urge to walk away, but instead I heard myself telling him that my father had been a farmer.

"I'm sorry if I'm overstepping, but can we talk to him?" the man said. "Personal stories will help bring attention to the problem."

"You can't. He killed himself twenty years ago."

The man turned pale, as if he suddenly felt ill. "I'm sorry," he said and just stood there, waiting for me to say more.

It started to snow. Weightless, like fluff.

"I came home one day to find a crowd around this big tree outside our house. People were staring at the three bodies hanging from the tree. My father, my mother, and my little sister."

My father had given up believing our lives would ever get better. I was almost seventeen when he sat me down to tell me his plan. He said if the four of us—the entire family—gave up our lives, that would send a message the government couldn't ignore. I didn't think he would actually go through with it.

A snowplow was spraying salt on the street in front of the mall. I shouldn't have gone on, but my story had started and wouldn't stop.

"My father's face had turned grey, his lungi was flapping in the wind. My mother's saree had come undone, and she looked so skinny with her midriff exposed. I couldn't bring myself to look at my sister's face, but I remember she was wearing a red dress that used to be mine. I don't know how they forced the noose around her neck. I don't know if my father did it or my mother. It was a jute rope. It must have been itchy on her," I said.

One of the neighbours helped me bring their bodies down. At the temple, the priest who came to do the puja for the funeral lit an entire pack of sandalwood agarbattis and a coconut oil lamp before the bodies were taken to the crematorium. The whole place smoked and stank of burning.

The man in the North Face jacket started to say something, but his voice cracked. A couple walking a chihuahua passed beside us. The dog strutted confidently, wearing tiny red boots, so sure of its safety.

I said, "I'll share your campaign on my Instagram."

He nodded briefly, like he thought I was small, with little influence. He probably thought I had a hundred or so followers—typical for a middle-aged coffee shop employee.

"I have 85,000 followers on Instagram," I blurted out. "I sell handmade peacock accessories. Many of my followers are my regular customers. Send me the link and I'll do a special sale and donate all the proceeds to the fundraiser."

I paused and then added, "Look for Peacocks of Instagram, no spaces."

The man said he would do so and got into his car. He didn't start the engine right away. I began to walk back to the café. The snow had already built up. Around me, people were waddling in it, trying not to fall, trying to catch buses, trying to get someplace warm. They probably had stories inside them, waiting to be released. Or holes inside them that would never be filled.

A blizzard howled in the distance. I would soon be home, with Kannan and his peafowl. With my closetful of beads and hooks and feathers. The snow pelted down sideways. Brutal. Beautiful.

Cake

MY NAILS WERE CHIPPED, a blistering maroon. I was standing in the corridor outside the general manager's office, where the lights were blinding and the carpet lush, my heart strained. My uniform reeked of urine—a mess from 801—but there was nothing I could do about it. If I didn't speak to him now, it would be too late.

Inside, Kron tried to make small talk—his Fourth of July weekend plans, this and that—but I knew this was how people like him distract you, so I got straight to the point.

"I came to ask for a promotion to housekeeping manager." There, I said it.

"I'm basically doing the job already since Peres got sick. Status reports, staff training, customer complaints."

Kron was blunt but also flattering. "I cannot lose our best housekeeper. You do what, twenty rooms a day? Do you know how many the average housekeeper does? Like twelve, or less!"

I stuck to my script. I retrieved the certificate from my pocket, flattened it, and slid it across his desk. "I completed an online hospitality management course."

Without glancing at it, his voice turning sour, Kron said, "Being a manager is a completely different thing."

Now I *really* had to get to the point. "My roommates are moving out soon. One is getting married, the other one is going back home, and I can't afford to pay the full rent. I've been looking for new roommates for months. No luck."

"Do you know QuickBooks? Skeduler? PowerPoint?" he said, each word a challenge.

"I'll pick them up quickly. I wanted to talk to you before you hired anyone else."

He stood up, grabbed his keys, and walked out the door. "I need to beat the traffic."

I knew not to run after him.

I could hear moaning coming from the room next door. I was wrapping the fitted sheet around the king-size mattress, my heart flattened to a wafer. It was late afternoon. What luxury to take time out of your workday to do that in a hotel room. The woman's moans swelled through the wall and lit a dull fire inside me. I wasn't finished with the bed, but I started the vacuum to drown out the fucking.

The vacuum cleaner hummed reliably, and I was lulled into a daydream. I read in a self-help book that you could *will* the things you wanted to happen by imagining them. I imagined the day I would leave my rat-ridden, decaying apartment for my very own gleaming townhouse at the edge of the city. The book said to make the wish vivid, like it was already happening. I was imagining the realtor giving me the keys, my belongings all packed in boxes, waiting for the moving van, when the vacuum cleaner gagged and stopped.

As I removed a clementine-sized hairball from the vacuum head, the woman climaxed and the man let out a grunt that was long and husky and grating.

In the silence that followed, I heard Kron's voice in the corridor. I peered through the peephole and saw an eager-looking man almost a foot shorter than Kron walking beside him toward the room where I was working.

As they neared the door, Kron's voice got louder. "We'll have your blazer ready on Monday. Welcome to Wyatt!" Then they made a right turn toward the elevators.

After that, I saw the man everywhere, running around like he was on fire. By the linen chute, at the front desk, in the maintenance room. Jasper was his name. His teeth were disorderly, like toilet paper rolls of different sizes shoved into a small space, but the whole arrangement made me feel something soft for him.

Soon, he started coming to me with questions. Simple questions, like what was a room status discrepancy. Or where to find a vendor contract. I asked him how the interview with Kron had gone, and he said with a laugh, "I have no idea how I got this job. I was the IT guy in another hotel, and I just applied for this on a whim. At the interview, I said some words I had googled minutes before, and right then, Kron handed me the job."

"So Kron didn't ask you about Skeduler or QuickBooks?"

"Not at all. I'm trying to figure them out. Can you help me?"

Jasper treated me like a friend, not a subordinate. Eye to eye. Shoulder to shoulder. In the bar one evening after my shift, he patted the stool beside him and asked me what I would like to drink. Cranberry juice, no ice. Mellowed by his merlot, he began to talk.

"I met my wife on the subway five years ago. She was sitting across from me, her legs crossed, engrossed in a book. I had never heard of the book, but she looked so beautiful that I said, 'Oh, I love that book.' She looked up at me and smiled. We talked the whole train ride. And since that day, she's clung onto me like lint," he said, chuckling a little, and then sighing. "But she takes good care of me."

"You know, you're very talented," he said unexpectedly. "What are you doing as a housekeeper?"

I shrugged.

"No, for real. You should be promoted. In fact, I think you should have my job. I'm going to speak to Kron."

I felt a stirring, like the first taste of something sweet.

Jasper said he would find a comparable job in the hotel for himself and convince Kron to give me his job. There was an opening for an IT manager, but it was a remote position. Jasper said he couldn't work from home. "I'd go crazy. My wife's home all day. She would give me no space."

"I thought you said your wife's very caring?"

"That's the problem, you see. It's hard to explain. She's just all over me when I'm home, and when I'm at work, she's texting me every hour. 'Did you eat? Did you take a break?'" He paused, studied the stem of his wineglass. "I know I should be grateful, but it's just too much. You understand, right?"

I felt sorry for him, the way you feel sorry for a dragon-fly with a crushed wing. I wondered if his wife knew how heavy her love was for him.

After we were done our drinks, he took the train with me. It was late evening, and the car was empty except for the two of us.

When his stop came, he said, "That's me," and quickly gave me a peck on the eyelid, leaving me dazed and throbbing.

• • •

Jasper called me in to work on my day off to help him schedule the Thanksgiving weekend. Staff would always take leave in hordes while the hotel was fully booked. He had me sit at the computer in his office. By the time we had figured out the schedule, I felt powerful and heady and hopeful.

Jasper kissed me and I kissed him back. And then we stopped and looked at each other with a new sadness.

He was taking two weeks off for Thanksgiving. His wife wanted to go to Vail. Jasper had convinced Kron to let me cover for him while he was away, give me his office, and relieve me from housekeeping duties. He even got me a blazer and a temporary name tag. The tag didn't have my name on it like the real ones, but it said: HOUSEKEEPING MANAGER. That was something. Soon, I would be free of cleaning other people's feces. I would have a decent place to stay. I would have money to visit my parents back home in Kozhikode.

Come see me in #320. I have a surprise for you, Jasper's text said.

I found him inside the suite, sipping wine. He had taken off his blazer and rolled up the sleeves of his white shirt. He had set up a little meal at the dining table: pasta, garlic bread, candles. The bottle of wine was already half-empty. The pasta was bland, and his conversation was filled with dread at having to spend two weeks with his wife.

After the meal, he pulled me up from my chair and started smelling my neck. He sighed, softly first, and then loudly. His arm grazed my back and slipped under my uniform.

I pulled away.

"Let's just have some fun, baby," he said, pulling me toward him and kissing my mouth. "I want you." His voice, a forceful whisper.

He unhooked my bra and squeezed my breasts from outside my shirt. Abruptly, he pushed me onto the bed and pulled down my pants. I wanted to run, to get out of that room and never return, but it required too much courage to pull myself away in that moment.

I thought about the name tag, and the cost of it.

Jasper went down on me and bit me. Hard. Then he flipped me over and pinned my arms down and entered me. I bit the blanket against the burning. He pulled out and came on my back. He got a towel from the bathroom and did a quick, careless wipe, leaving my skin sticky.

I slipped into the bathroom and locked the door. The burning would not stop.

Jasper knocked on the door and said, "You okay? I'm heading downstairs."

"Yeah," I said.

"Just clean up the room, okay?" The door crashed a few seconds later.

During Thanksgiving week I walked around with something bigger than me lodged painfully in my windpipe, like a watermelon stretching out a translucent stocking. I threw myself into the new role as if that was the only way I could manage a few sips of air.

I steamed my new blazer and put on lipstick. I introduced the use of personal notes to collect guest feedback and special requests. These requests were mostly easy asks. Don't tuck in the blanket. Leave extra coffee pods, extra towels. Deal with messes quickly. That sort of thing. I personally checked whether they were fulfilled. The housekeeping staff got better tips, and the hotel got a bunch of good reviews, a rare thing for Thanksgiving weekend.

Kron said, "Someone's getting recognized at the holiday party."

Jasper ended up taking one more week off, but he was back for the party. He was there with his wife, who leaned her petite, wispy frame against him as he leaned away from her. I wore a dress I found at a thrift store, green velvet with baggy, lingering sleeves that made me look out of place, like a farm animal in a zoo. Sales, Marketing, Corporate, hotel staff, everyone was there with their families. The president of the hotel chain gave the keynote speech. Then it was time to honour the high performers. Names and pictures appeared on the screen as the president read out their accomplishments. Kron was recognized for leading the location with the highest growth in revenue.

"And next, in housekeeping excellence," the president said, "at a time when we historically receive complaints and negative reviews, one location managed to turn things around and set an example. One of our colleagues, house-keeping manager—" he paused, looking at the screen, which still showed Kron. "Sorry, I didn't change the slide. Okay, there we go."

The image flipped to a portrait of Jasper, standing side-ways with his arms crossed, smiling broadly. The president kept talking, but my ears stopped co-operating. I stared at Jasper's picture, my elbows on the table. I studied his teeth, the many different shapes of them. I studied the faces and bodies of all the people staring at his picture and something venomous rose in me.

I went over to Kron's table, where Jasper and his wife were also seated.

"I need to talk to you," I said.

"Yes, of course, my dear, but could you please grab some warm water with lemon for Mrs. Venn here?" He smiled at Jasper's wife.

I stood there, unable to move, and Jasper's wife, this Mrs. Venn, said, "It's just that my throat is sensitive to iced water. Sorry for the trouble."

I went to the kitchen and put the kettle on, then found a lemon and cut two slices. The fabric of my dress caught the edge of the counter and ripped in an L-shape at my hip. When I delivered the water and lemon to the table, Kron was nowhere to be seen.

In a treacly voice, while removing a piece of lint from her husband's suit, Mrs. Venn said, "Thanks so much."

Later, I found Mrs. Venn contemplating the desserts at the buffet table. "So many options!" she exclaimed. "Do you know what's good?"

"The cheesecake's great," I said.

"They all look so good," she said, still surveying the selection like she had all the time in the world.

I served myself a piece of cheesecake and was about to walk away, but I stopped. "How was your vacation?" I asked Mrs. Venn.

"It was just heavenly. The mountains, the restaurants, the trails." She finally decided on the cheesecake, put a piece on her plate, and took a bite. Making an orgasmic face, she squealed, "Oh, my word! This is so good." She ate daintily, chewing like a squirrel. "I'm so sad to be back now. And I don't want to loan Jasp back to the hotel. You know how hard he works."

I noticed Jasper watching us. He dropped his napkin on the table and started walking toward us. I knew I had to be quick.

"There's a new position opening at the hotel," I told Mrs. Venn. "IT manager. It's work-from-home, too. Jasper's worked in IT, right?"

"Oh my goodness, yes, that's what he did at Orchids."

Jasper joined us and, looking at his wife's plate, said, "Good choice."

"Honey, did you hear? There's a work-from-home opening in IT! You should talk to Kron and get *that* job."

Jasper's face turned a shocking shade of dusk, his forehead contorted in bewilderment.

"This is such wonderful news," Mrs. Venn said to me. "We're planning to have a baby, and this would work out great for us." She started walking back to their table with Jasper in tow, saying, "Kron's back. Let's talk to him."

I took a large bite of cake and let it melt in my mouth as I watched the scene unfold at their table.

Kron took away the temporary name tag and replaced it with a personalized one. Embossed on thick brass, this one read:

RANIA ALI

HOUSEKEEPING MANAGER

That weekend, I got my nails done. I asked for multicoloured tips like the ladies at the front desk had. The woman at the salon was quiet as she removed years of hardened cuticle, building a little pile of skin as if for a science experiment. She shaped my nails into neat ovals and painted them clear with tips that were many shades of pink. When the lacquer was completely dry, she put some lotion on my hands and massaged them. My nails sparkled under the salon's fluorescence as my eyes burned.

Whatever Happened,
Happened for the Good

WE ARE HERE FOR Ma's new kidney.

Here, everyone looks like us, but somehow, I feel superior, in a way I never do back home in Canada. People stare at me like they think I am special. My grandfather—silver-haired Appoopa, in his white shirt and mundu—is waiting at the airport outside a black Ambassador taxi. Appoopa sits in the front with the driver, and Ma, Dad, and I get in the back. I sink into the red leather and Dad looks for the seat belt. There is none. The front seat of the car is continuous, with no cupholders. A bus-like car. A car like bus. There is no air conditioning, so we roll down the windows, turning the manual crank, letting in the heavy, sticky May air.

We drive past the manicured Trivandrum airport gardens onto a road where the divider swells with green. Appoopa speaks to me like I am five, though I am already eight. He says to Ma, "Molay, don't worry about k-i-d-n-e-y. We'll figure it out." He doesn't realize that I learned to spell years ago.

All at once, an intense fishy smell hits us, and I feel something coming up from my stomach to my throat. I swallow it. The taxi driver announces, "This is Shankumugham Beach." The road bends and the beach appears suddenly, the thick emerald-green trees giving way to white sand. People crowd the shoreline with their pants rolled up or sarees raised, letting the giant foamy waves chase them.

"What a giant lake," I say.

"It's not a lake, Raji, it's the Arabian Sea," Ma says.

"Can we go there one day?" I say, smiling the way I smile to get Ma to do things for me, my cheeks touching my eyes.

"Of course," Ma says. "I'll plan a trip with everyone. Ammu, Unni, Suchi, everyone."

Lately, my mother has been pretending everything is fine and she can do all the things she used to. When she first got the news about her kidneys, she shut herself in her bedroom. Dad went to her, and I curled up in my room and pretended to read. They emerged after a few hours, Ma's eyeballs pink. It wasn't the first time I'd seen her cry, but it was the first time I saw that terrified look on her face. Dad and I were the ones who were always scared of things—cockroaches, roller coasters, airplane turbulence—but Ma was never afraid of anything. Until now.

She was bitter for weeks and went on an investigative mission to find out how she had got this rare disease. There was no family history, no underlying physical condition; her diet was always healthy. As if she would be able to accept it if there were a reason for it.

Now, three years in, she laughs about it. Mostly. When she meets someone new, she wants to know how good or bad their kidneys are. She'll see someone walking down the street, or someone complaining about something normal, like the weather or taxes, and she'll say, "I bet they have great kidneys." It's like when you compliment a friend for something they have, like a pool or a puppy, but you really just want it for yourself.

She told her friends in Canada that she was going to India to get a new and improved kidney. They laughed at her wit, despite knowing that the chances of finding a match are low and that a transplant only buys you an additional ten to twelve years. That would make me around twenty and my mother forty-five. Best case.

The taxi driver points out landmarks like the naked Jalakanyaka Mermaid statue, the museum, the zoo, Kowdiar Palace, and several temples. Attached to the car's dashboard is a small bronze statue of Lord Shiva, like the one we have back home. Each time we pass a temple, the driver touches his forehead and his chest and mutters something under his breath.

He turns into the narrow, pothole-ridden road leading to my grandparents' home in Indira Nagar. Their house sits at a busy intersection right where the main road forks into two lanes. It is flat roofed, with mouldy walls that were once pinkish-purple. A low wall encloses the house. There is a red and white gate with a red mailbox affixed to it. On the wall beside the gate is a metal plate engraved with the name Jyothis. Over the years, Ma has referred to this house, the one she grew up in, by its name, as if it were a family member.

The driver honks as we pull up to the gate. My cousins race out to open it. The driveway is short, and the back of the taxi sticks out of the property. Ma's younger sister, Suchi Aunty, and her kids, Ammu and Unni, who live with my grandparents, welcome us with glowing smiles. Ammu is my age, Unni a few years younger. Behind them is my grandmother—Ammooma, who is just a little taller than me. When she smiles, the mounds of her cheeks touch her eyelashes. She has a dimpled chin that cradles her round face. It is my chin, too, and Ma's and Suchi Aunty's and Ammu's. I have seen Ammooma twice before, when I was one and then when I was three, but I don't remember much about those visits. Ma tells me to hug her, and I wrap my arms around her generous waist. Ammu is wearing a cotton dress that she has outgrown; the hem falls inches above her knees to reveal some seriously admirable scars. Unni is wearing a button-down checkered shirt with the sleeves carelessly rolled up. I feel childish in my jean overalls and Mary Janes.

Suchi Aunty locks Ma in a long, embarrassing embrace. She looks like my mother but messier. Her hair is frizzy, her shoulders droopy, her body round. Ma is leaner and stands straighter; her hair is styled, and she wears heels with her jeans. Suchi Aunty is wearing a floral cotton nightie, as if it's something normal to wear in the afternoon. She releases Ma, and then hugs her again. I can't tell if she's smiling or crying.

After a lunch of rice, dal, papadum, yam fry, and fish curry, with everything tasting of coconut, Ammu and Unni give me a tour of the outside of the house. The yard has no lawn, but it is engorged with greenery. We circle the property: past the bright periwinkle plants; the palm trees whose coconuts, high in the air, look like coffee beans bunched together; the jackfruit trees with their bursting, lumpy fruit, each the size of a human baby; the unruly hibiscus plants; the mango tree that has stopped bearing mangoes; and Ammooma's custard apple tree. In the backyard there's a washing stone—a cube of concrete with a rough surface. Crow shit is splattered across it like a cluster of eyes—white blots with black pupils. A narrow concrete groove encircles the property, carrying rainwater, dead leaves, and crushed millipedes into the big drain outside the gate.

From the stories my mother has told me, I expected her family to be different. More noise, more laughter, more fun.

But the mood here is grim, like school after the teacher yells at the entire class because a few kids were rowdy. Over lunch, the women talk and talk and talk about Ma's condition and everything she went through back in Canada. How her health kept deteriorating as she waited for specialist appointments and diagnostic procedures. How she was finally admitted to the hospital because she had collapsed. How it was too late, her kidneys had already failed. All the blood in her body was passing through her broken kidneys.

In those early days, she would say, "I can't eat anything I like. Everything I love—mangoes, cheese, potatoes, tomatoes, chocolate—out of the question."

She looked sad whenever she entered the kitchen, as if the loss of taste was worse than the loss of an organ. She would still make me the food I liked: pasta with cheese sauce, noodles with tomato sauce, or chocolate chip cookies. I felt bad for her, so I started telling her I liked the food she was eating. I would sit with her and have Cream of Wheat, or steamed veggies with no salt, or plain oatmeal, which tasted like a freshly opened glue stick—don't ask me how I knew this—but I didn't want her to feel alone.

When we were invited to parties, my mother would bring her own container of snacks or a bottle of cranberry juice. If someone offered her wine, she declined, saying, "I have grapes, which is basically the same thing." This made everyone laugh and put them at ease.

It has been three years. Three pretzel-shaped years. Ma has been on dialysis, waiting for a kidney. All the blood in her body filtered by a machine outside her. At night I could hear Ma and Dad talking through the thin wall that separates my room from theirs. Most transplants come from family or friends. Dad was not a match, and we didn't have any family or friends in Canada close enough to ask for a kidney. I told Ma she could take one of mine, but her eyes welled and she said I was too young for that.

Sometime at the beginning of all this, Ma sat me down and asked, "Raji, are you okay? Are you feeling bad about all this? My health?"

I pretended I didn't know what she was talking about, but my eyes, those unreliable things, betrayed me, and I burst out crying like a world-class wuss. Ma's face turned stoic. She pulled me close to her chest and held me there. One thing about Ma is that her hands are always ice cold, which isn't great for a nurse.

The day after we arrive, Ma, Dad, and Appoopa leave for the new hospital. Ammooma takes me with her to the market, which she calls "chanda." I laugh when she says this because it sounds like another word my cousins use: "chandi," which means buttocks. When Ammooma laughs, her belly jiggles under her saree.

We take two buses to get to the market. Outside, two gaping potholes filled with days-old rainwater welcome us. A buffalo with pink horns sits in the middle of one of the potholes, soaking in the water, ignoring the massive blue-bottles hovering over it.

Ammooma mumbles, her face scrunched up, "Why can't this filthy animal find someplace else to laze in?"

I say, "Because the market is a butt." Ammooma giggles again.

Once we get past the entrance, the buffalo stench gives way to fish stench, which is far more potent. There are so many vegetable stalls, followed by fish stalls, all tightly packed in a haphazard fashion. At each stall, however, there is meticulous order. Pyramids of oranges, apples, and tomatoes. Tidy heaps of okra, green beans, and other vegetables I have never seen before. Ammooma breaks the tips of okra to test their freshness and squeezes the tomatoes to test their ripeness.

The fish stalls are organized, with each type of fish stacked in neat piles, their heads pointing north and tails pointing south, arranged from smallest to largest. Ammooma says the smallest ones smell the worst.

The fish vendor is a thin man with shiny skin and bright teeth. He repeats the names of the fish in singsong.

"Aila ... Chala ... Para ... Chura ... Naimeen ..."

"Aila ... Chala ... Para ... Chura ... Naimeen ..."

"Aila ... Chala ... Para ... Chura ... Naimeen ..."

The fish lie still like mimes playing dead, their mouths half-open, their eyes all looking in the same direction.

As we wait for the bus to go home, Ammooma and I each hold a bag. The buses are overflowing with passengers hanging from the open doors. Yet somehow, more people get on. But not Ammooma. She wants to wait for a bus where we can sit. I am so relieved.

The private buses have names and are painted in bright colours. Meena, Al Ameen, Annie Mol pass by, their insides packed. After waiting for half an hour, we get on Shaji. Ammooma and I find seats in the middle of the bus. The wind carries the metallic smell of betel juice. An old woman sits in front of us chewing, her lips bright orange against her dark skin. The bus speeds past a white building, which Ammooma tells me is the Secretariat, where the state government sits. The man behind us sticks his head out the window to look at students protesting in front of the building.

The old woman spits out her betel juice against the wind. Ammooma sees it coming and pulls me close to her, but the man behind us gets sprayed all over his face.

The man yells at the old woman and wipes his face with a handkerchief.

She yells back, "Who asked you to stick your head out the window?" She turns to look at us and asks me, "You're not from here, right?"

I don't know how she can tell, but I say, "From Canada."

"I knew it when I heard you speak," she says. She continues to stare at me, like she's observing an animal in the zoo. Then she says, "My granddaughter has a beauty spot in her eye, like you."

I've always hated that black spot in the white of my right eye—it looks like someone poked me with a permanent marker.

The woman adds, "I think it means you'll have a long life. Or a short life. I can't remember."

Ammooma tells the woman to mind her own business.

By the time we get home, my parents are back from the hospital.

Ma tells Ammooma, "He's such a good doctor. Unlike any doctor I have met in Canada in the twelve years I have been there. So sensible, he spent an hour talking to me, asking questions in detail. He says my case is idiopathic, meaning cause unknown." She sighs, and I wonder if she is satisfied with the explanation that there is no explanation. "Not just him. The nurse, the reception staff, the techs, everyone was so kind. You get the feeling that they really care. I guess that's what happens when you can buy health care. They got me to do all the blood work, ultrasound, everything in the same day. I should have just come here right from the beginning."

Ammooma and Appoopa grasp at every tiny positive piece of news. Dad and I used to be like that, but we have seen Ma get worse and better and worse over the past three years, so we are cautious with our hope.

One time, I was still awake when she came back from the hospital after dialysis. Through the wall, I heard her crying and heaving. "Naren, I don't want Raji to remember me like this," she said, "like a sick patient."

Now I look at everyone here as a potential kidney donor. Appoopa, Ammooma, Suchi Aunty, Ma's cousins who visited—they all look like kidneys to me. Bean-shaped, life-giving masses.

It has been a week since we arrived, but I am still jet-lagged. Dad is back to normal. Ma says she's a tough old bird, she doesn't get jet-lagged. She says it often:

"I'm a tough old bird, I drove myself to the hospital when I was in labour."

"I'm a tough old bird, I haven't gotten a cold in five years."

"I'm a tough old bird, I can't be slowed down by a silly kidney disease."

Unlike Ma, Suchi Aunty gets very nervous when she suffers from even a slight cold. She works at a bank, but it seems like she doesn't make very much money. When

Ammu or Unni ask her for something, she says she will buy it for them after she gets her next paycheque. If they protest, she says, "Who do you think I work for? A Saudi sheikh?"

My cousins laugh like they don't give a hoot about getting scolded. Not a trace of guilt or shock or regret.

Suchi Aunty's husband left when the kids were toddlers. Still, she credits their good looks to him. "Thank goodness they look like him. They wouldn't get too far looking like this," she says, making a circle around her face with her finger.

Suchi Aunty looks like Ma, but she doesn't have a happy face. She has an always-tired face, eyes hollow and cheeks puffy. And she has a strange affliction: every night, her right eye closes involuntarily. She will be watching TV in the living room or eating at the dining table, and at 9 p.m. sharp, her right eye will shut and remain like that until the next morning.

It is June, but the monsoons are late.

"I'm sure I'll be a match," Ammooma says to Ma. She is standing in the backyard, soaping clothes on the washing stone. She has wrapped the loose end of her saree around herself and tucked it into the waist. "Our neighbour's niece gave a kidney to her sixteen-year-old daughter, and both of them are fine now."

"I hope there won't be any complications for you, Amma," Ma says with a sigh, her forehead creased.

"Everything will be fine, molay. I have broken coconuts at Padmanabhaswamy temple for you," Ammooma says, and I wonder what that has to do with anything. But Ma's eyes brighten, as if the coconuts give her energy.

Ma separates the whites from the rest of the laundry and puts them into a bucket. "I'll do these," she says. She sets the bucket under the tap and fills it to the brim.

"Go and sit inside," Ammooma says. "You shouldn't be lifting anything heavy."

Ma relents and goes into the house. I sit on the stone steps and wrap my arms around my knees. "Ammooma, why don't you use the washing machine?" I ask.

"It uses too much electricity, and half the time we don't have power," Ammooma replies in a quick, mumbling-grumbling tone. "And besides, the machine never gets the laundry as clean as stone washing does." She sets the bucket of whites beside the stone, opens a small blue bottle, and adds a few drops of purple liquid to the water.

"What's that?" I ask.

"Ujala," she says. "It will make the whites whiter."

"But it's making them blue."

"After washing, they will become white," she says, wiping sweat off her brow with the back of her hand.

I wonder if Ma will get Ammooma's traits if she gets

her kidney. It's weird to think that my mother might carry a piece of her mother inside her. Like how she was inside her mother at one point. I asked Dad what happens to the person giving the kidney, and he said people can easily live with one kidney. Isn't it strange that we have two of something when we need only one?

July comes and goes. Ma is in pain most of the time, exhausted after her visits to the hospital. The visits are costing my parents a lot of money. I've never heard them talk about spending money at the hospital back in Canada. I think about my piggy bank stuffed with quarters and loonies and feel bad that I didn't bring it along.

Ma, Dad, and I sleep in the same bed in one of the two bedrooms in Jyothis. Ammooma, Suchi Aunty, Ammu, and Unni sleep in the other bedroom, and Appoopa sleeps on the diwan in the living room. One night, I hear Ma tell Dad she is worried about how losing a kidney will affect Ammooma's health because of her age. I want to tell Ma that she doesn't need to worry about Ammooma, who can take buses and go to the market by herself, haggle with vendors and carry heavy bags of groceries, wash more laundry than the washing machine, and cook up a feast so quickly.

• • •

Ammooma is not a match.

With red eyes and quivering lips—her trying-not-to-cry-face—she says to Ma, "I couldn't even do that for you."

I don't know why she says this because she does things for people all day long.

That night, Ma is rolled into a ball at the edge of the bed, her criss-crossed arms wrapped around her criss-crossed legs and her face buried between her chest and her knees. She doesn't even care that I am awake, sitting at her feet on the cool terracotta floor.

Dad sits down in front of her and says, "Hema, you have to stay strong."

From behind her knees, Ma's voice is both muffled and echoey. "My creatinine is getting worse every day. I don't want to die like this."

"We won't let you die. We'll find a way." Dad's voice is not confident, even I can hear it.

"I feel like my body hates me. Everything hurts, Naren."

"You'll get better soon, Hema. You're at the finish line. We'll find a donor, but you need to keep the faith."

Ma lifts her head and stares at nothing in particular, her eyes dry as if she doesn't even have the strength to cry. I wrap my arms around the whole ball of her, but she just stays there, unaffected, as if she were all alone.

• • •

Appoopa is not a match either.

Ma isn't as upset as she was when we found out about Ammooma; it's almost as if she expected this. Later that night, I hear Ammooma tell Suchi Aunty that a sibling would probably match because they share the same genes.

"My kids only have me. I can't afford to give my kidney away," Suchi Aunty says.

Ma hears her, too. I know because I hear a whimper and then a long sigh. I cross off Suchi Aunty from my dwindling kidney-donor list, suddenly hating the nasal, murmuring sound of her voice.

After that, my mother develops a strange sense of calm. She advocates for the cause of organ donation. She has everyone in the family fill out forms signing up to be organ donors. She prays a lot. She reads the Bhagavad Gita and translates quotes she wants me to understand:

Whatever happened, happened for the good;
Whatever is happening, is happening for the good;
Whatever will happen, will also happen for the good.

I wonder if she believes it.

Ammooma takes Ma to an astrologer, who tells her there is a severe Shani Dosham in Ma's birth chart. Saturn is in the wrong place. There is a pariharam. A remedy. Do a Ganapathi homam in the house, clear all the bad energy, and then go to this remote temple in Kochi and tie a whole, unhusked coconut onto a pillar there.

The priest who comes to Jyothis to do the homam removes his shirt, folds it neatly, and puts it into a Bhima Jewellers shopping bag. A few strands of white hair curl up around his nipples and in the dip of his chest. He sets up a small square structure using bricks, fills it with sand, then pieces of wood, and pours ghee into it. He lights a fire and starts praying in Sanskrit. Crows caw non-stop.

Ma's cousins and some neighbours show up. There's a feast, a full-blown sadya—parippu, sambar, avial, rasam, thoran, injicurry, two types of payasams, upperi—the whole shebang. Everyone is careful not to look too happy. Afterward, Ma packs our bags for Kochi with a closed-mouth expression like she burned her tongue.

We are all waiting, holding our breath, afraid to move.

At the train station, a breeze carries a barrage of smells—sandalwood incense, sambar from the canteen, sewage from the open drains, talcum powder. A tall man wearing a faded tank top and shorts, and carrying a backpack longer than his torso, stands by the Frooti stall. There is a Canadian flag patch on his backpack. Beside him and wearing similar clothes, a woman nearly as tall pays for a bottle of Bisleri water.

The shopkeeper, a small man, asks, "Madam, tea, coffee?"

She shakes her head and asks the man with the backpack, "How many hours to Kochi?" She pronounces it "coachee."

Without looking at her, he replies, "'Bout five."

I suddenly feel a longing for home, an urgency to get back to Canada, as if I have no idea how I ended up in this strange place.

Ma, Dad, and Suchi Aunty stand with me on the platform. It is only 9 a.m., but it is already sticky. Suchi Aunty fans her face with the pallu of her saree as sweat soaks the back of her blouse. Ma is in a trance. I think she is praying with her eyes wide open.

A crow caws in threes. *Caw caw caw*. Pause. *Caw caw caw*.

We hear a rumble in the distance and feet begin to shuffle. A swarm of people charges toward the edge of the platform. Among them is a little girl—the size of a five-year-old but behaving like an adult—in a dusty, oversized shirt and a long skirt. She extends her hand, maintaining eye contact with one passenger at a time. Some of them drop change into her palm, which she promptly puts into a maroon cloth bag hanging across her body. As the rumble grows louder, making everything else inaudible, Ma fiddles with her purse, watching the approaching train. She hands a five-rupee note to the girl, who smiles at her with much brightness.

Suchi Aunty says, "Don't encourage her. They will all start hounding you."

The train slows and screeches to a stop. Dad helps me up and we find seats. The little girl has also entered the train and is making quick rounds of the aisles. At the end of our aisle sits an elderly man, his button-down shirt stretching, showing holes of stomach. A vendor approaches, calling out in sing-song, "Kaapi, kaapi, kaapi." The man calls the vendor and makes a "V" sign, sticking out two fingers. The vendor pours coffee into a clay cup; the man pulls out his wallet and pays.

The train hoots. The vendor and the little girl expertly exit as it begins to move. The train whizzes past the sign THIRUVANANTHAPURAM CENTRAL, the platform disappears, and the city emerges, revealing a large red cylindrical building with the words INDIAN COFFEE HOUSE affixed to the top. As the train picks up speed, the city becomes a blur.

It happens so quick.

The screech of metal. Screams. Suitcases and loose items from plastic bags falling over our heads. Bodies dropping and turning. The train flips, and our bodies and bags are dragged to one end. Part of a wall caves in and my fore-arm cracks. I am on top of a bunch of people. Something snaps and a broken piece of metal thrusts toward me. I duck behind a large backpack and close my eyes.

When everything comes to a halt, I hear wailing. A wall with windows is on the ground, and the floor of the train lies to our side. I sit up from my spot behind the backpack with the Canadian flag on it. The tall man is lying beside me. He tries to stand up, his bare knees bloody. I desperately want the splitting pain in my arm to stop.

All my family survives that afternoon, except Suchi Aunty. She dies in the hospital, along with eleven other people. I get a cast around my arm. Within a few hours, the doctors wheel Ma into the operating room for the transplant. They end up transplanting both of Suchi Aunty's kidneys, as they are of no use to her anymore. They also take out her heart valve, liver, and pancreas—everything she indicated on the organ bank form.

When we get back to Jyothis, Dad is the one who tells Ammu and Unni that their mother has died. He keeps it short and fast, matter-of-fact. It is not easy for him, I can tell, because his shoulders are rounded and his voice sounds like he has a cold.

The priest from last week is back. Suchi Aunty, wrapped in a white cloth, lies on the living room floor. He lights a pack of incense sticks and pushes them into a banana. The sandalwood smell is intense and smoky, forbidding any other smells to emerge. We sit cross-legged around Suchi Aunty for hours as the priest chants prayers.

Tears run down my face without stopping. I hold Ammu's hand with my good hand, hoping she knows what I would like to tell her—that I'm sorry her mother died, sorry my mother will live because of it. She hangs her head and looks at the red terracotta floor. Unni does not stop crying and insists on resting his face on Suchi Aunty's chest. She has a large scar over her nose and upper lip. It looks like the flesh was ripped off and someone tried to put it back together.

A week after Suchi Aunty dies, Ammooma returns to the kitchen. Her belly doesn't jiggle with laughter, and she doesn't wear her goofy smile anymore. She cooks rice, dal, and long beans with shredded coconut. She puts small portions of the food on a banana leaf and places it on the washing stone in the backyard.

Crows create a ruckus.

"Why did you put the food there?" I ask Ammooma.

"It's for Suchi. She'll come back as a crow. We should give her food every day so she will come visit us."

A glossy black crow swoops down and begins to feast on the food.

Ammooma says, "That's Suchi. How beautiful and shiny!"

Within a few minutes, three crows are feasting on the food. Ammooma looks intently at the birds. A fourth crow joins them and Ammooma runs at it, shouting, "Disgusting Vella Kaka!"

"Why did you shoo that one away?" I ask her.

"It was a white crow," she says.

"The crow looked black to me," I say gently.

She says, "Its neck was grey, not black."

"What's wrong with a white crow?"

"Suchi would never come back as a white crow. Only bad people—infidels—come back as white crows," she says. "Suchi saved your mother's life. She is immortal."

I think back to all the crows I've seen since arriving here, never noticing a difference, imagining them as good people and bad people, coming back to visit the homes they were forced to leave. Immortals and infidels.

Whatever happened, happened for the good. Good for whom?

By the end of August, it is decided. We will stay in India to help raise Ammu and Unni. We rent a house near Jyothis, and they move in with us, our family suddenly so big.

Ma's new kidneys are top-notch, filtering her blood effortlessly. But she is different now. Nurses make very little money here, we find out. She works at a busy clinic and comes home each evening tired in her bones, changes into her cotton nightie, and cooks for us. She lets her hair run curly and grey. And her right eye closes after dinner. She walks around like that, with one eye shut, until she goes to bed.

At Christmas, there is no tree and no snow. Dad buys a

single star, hangs a light bulb inside it, and suspends it from the porch ceiling, like all the other houses on the street.

I ask Ma about presents.

"Who do you think I work for?" she says. "A Saudi sheikh?"

Live-In

THE MICROWAVE DINGS AND my father says, "It's so quiet, even the dogs don't bark here." And then he begins to cough again.

"You should have let me get you health insurance," I say, making a mental note to look for options later. My sister, Paru, shrugs and purses her lips, frustrated by the incompetence of her father and brother.

My father's hair is greyer than the last time I saw him, three years ago. Now I realize I look so much like him—the same square face, the same thick hair, nearly the same height.

"This is just a throat irritation. And I'm only here for a month," he says. "Besides, this insurance business is a scam. You pay to get sick? What nonsense!"

Back in India, my father has been going to the same doctor for forty years, paying him a few hundred rupees (a couple thousand when he feels generous) for each visit. Twice, he had to have surgery—once an angioplasty and another a heart bypass—which he paid for from his savings.

"Appa, the medical bills here are not like in India," Paru says. She and her family flew in from New Jersey yesterday. "If something happens ..." she says, folding the throw blanket on the back of the couch. She is always doing something with her hands, like our mother used to.

"Nothing will happen," he says. "You people have everything, but you're still worried about what can go wrong. When you were both small, we had so little, living in that small house, but we managed everything smiling." He starts to cough again, stops, and says, "No worry, nothing."

"All I'm saying is that it's better to be safe than sorry," Paru says. "One of my friend's mother had this weird infection on her toe, and they ended up spending like three thousand dollars on doctor's visits."

"She should have taken her toe back to India. These people here have all the facilities but don't know how to give service to people. Back in the day, people used to go to America for treatment. Now everyone is coming to India. Our neighbour's uncle, who lives in Chicago, he came to KIMS hospital in Kerala for a knee replacement," my father says, his voice swelling with pride. "Even Canada is the same."

"Come on, Appa, they have universal health care," Paru says.

"I am all for socialism. I used to be a communist, too, back in my college days. But when you have to wait and wait and wait, you get tired." I remember a photo of my father back in his youth, striking a pose in front of the Secretariat building in Trivandrum holding a red flag with a hammer and a sickle. The older you get, the more lifetimes you live.

"Krishna Aunty's son had a cyst in his kidney. He makes a lot of money, but he couldn't get a nephrologist appointment in Canada for six months. What if his kidney explodes? He came to Fortis in Delhi, and in two weeks, cyst removed, all done." My father fans out his hands, indicating finality.

When neither of us speak, my father continues, "And remember Raji's mom, Hema? Why did they move to India? Hema had that kidney problem, and they were waiting for a transplant in Canada for years. She would have died if she hadn't come back."

Paru says, "I haven't heard from Raji is ages. How is she? And Ammu and Unni?"

The mention of Raji stirs me, and I remember that she appeared in a dream a few weeks after I proposed to my fiancée, Samantha. Raji and her cousins, Ammu and Unni, were our neighbours back in Indira Nagar. Raji and I were in the same grade at the same school, and I loved her for many years, believing she loved me, too. But before we left for different colleges, I professed my love for her, and she said she liked me a lot but was confused about what she wanted, who she was. We didn't speak much after that. It took me a long while to get over her.

"Raji's still in Bangalore. Her husband is working somewhere in the US. Ammu and Unni are still home. Ammu works for that bank, and Unni is studying for the civil service examination. He tried twice before but didn't pass. I think he'll get it this time. He's such a hard worker. For a child who lost his mother and never really had a father, it's no small feat. Imagine Unni as an IAS officer," my father says, spelling out each letter of the Indian Administrative Service acronym. "He's a good kid, always ready to help. He takes good care of Hema, too, who still has a bunch of health problems."

"Raji's in Bangalore, and her husband is here?" I ask.

"Yeah, that's what I heard. I think she had a baby recently and has a nice job she doesn't want to leave," my father says.

I wonder if Raji is happy.

"I'm starving," Paru says, taking out her phone. "I'm ordering pizza."

"I don't want pisa again," my father says.

"Do you want Indian?" Paru says, scrolling on her phone. "Like avial and sambar?"

"No, like butter chicken and naan."

"I don't want that greasy North Indian stuff. Do they

have Kerala food? I feel like having chemmeen curry. Haven't
had it in a long time."

"There is a Kerala restaurant about forty-five minutes
from here, but they don't deliver," I say.

"No, no, pisa is fine then. Anyway, nobody can match
your mother's chemmeen curry," my father says, sighing.
"You know her secret? Fresh coconut milk."

Our mother used to break coconuts open in our backyard,
grate the flesh, and squeeze it through a muslin cloth to make
coconut milk. I haven't thought about that since she died.

"Paru, how about Thai?" I say, scrolling through my
phone. "Appa, I want to take you to this Thai place downtown. I think you'll like it. They have coconut—"

"Not now. After the wedding. No time for all that now,"
he says, and stops a cough that started to grate in his throat.
He looks around, restless. "Can you connect my phone to
the internet? I have to remind Unni to water your mother's
plants." He still calls them our mother's plants, as if she's
just gone away for a short time.

He hands me his phone. It has no passcode. I find my
Wi-Fi on the list of available networks and enter the pass-
word. A bunch of notifications pop up. Most of them are
messages from Unni. He was still in high school when I
left home all those years ago, someone I barely paid any
attention to. Now, in his profile picture, he is wearing a tight
red T-shirt, his biceps showing. I am tempted to read the

messages. There are many. Unni is asking if my father has reached the US safely. He's saying that he watered the indoor plants but not the outdoor ones because it has been raining heavily. Something about a wilting banana tree. He's sent some pictures of himself and his friends at Shankumugham Beach. I remember lying to my father in college and going to that very beach with my friends. I scroll up the slew of recent messages from Unni to see the ones my father sent him. In one message he is telling Unni not to worry about his exams, that he will do well. In another, he is making a joke about the prime minister.

There's an ease between them that I have never experienced with my father. His texts to me are a lot less frequent and a lot more formal, asking about my work or travel plans, telling me about renovations at home, or births, or deaths of people he knows. Unni has sent him a meme of a golden retriever puppy sitting in the driver's seat of a car, holding on to the steering wheel saying, *I have no idea what I'm doing*. My father has responded: OMG, followed by three heart-eye emojis. This lands on my chest like the dull pain after a workout.

Paru's seven-year-old son runs into the room and asks my father if he wants to go out with him and his dad. My father has trouble understanding his American accent and the fast way he speaks.

"Appa, do you want to go outside with them?" Paru says.

"For what?"

"Just a walk. You've been inside since yesterday."

"Fine, fine. I'll come. Wait."

Paru and I watch the three of them walk onto the crescent-shaped sidewalk, past the driveway and the garbage can brimming with pizza boxes. The cul-de-sac is sunny and stark. Our father, in his khadi shirt and formal pants, stands out like an antique at IKEA. He lives alone in our old house in Trivandrum. I want him to move here with me, but it is difficult for me to ask him. For many reasons. One, it would be admitting to him that I don't think he can take care of himself for much longer. Two, I don't know how Samantha would react. We've never spoken explicitly about it, although she did say once that she would support me in whatever way I wanted to help my father. Still, I cannot imagine the two of them living in the same house. I cannot imagine reconciling the two versions of myself—the obedient, dutiful, reverent son, and the potty-mouthed, cheeky, impulsive boyfriend.

"Okay, so the gift bags are all ready," Paru says. "You want them in the rooms, right?"

"Just drop them off at the Wyatt concierge. Ask for the manager, Rania. She'll take care of everything."

"You guys have to be more careful," Paru says, retrieving a lipstick from her pocket. "I found *this* in the guest bedroom."

When I first told my father about Samantha, he asked me if she was North Indian. I told him she was mixed, with a white father and a Gujarati mother. He sighed and said, "In that case, it's better the wedding is outside of India." He didn't even insist on a South Indian wedding. Samantha has a big family here, from both sides, so I've gone to great lengths to invite a number of my friends from across North America.

"So, walk me through the events once more," Paru says.

"Today, we'll drop off the gift bags. Tomorrow evening, we'll have the Mehndi at Samantha's parents' place, and the rehearsal dinner at the Wyatt. Then the Baraat and the wedding are the day after, with the reception in the evening and brunch the next day."

"What do we have to do for the Baraat?"

"I guess I'll climb up onto the horse and everyone from our side will start dancing to the music," I say, and Paru makes a face like she is already embarrassed.

"How long do we have to dance?" she asks, starkly revealing the South Indian in her who doesn't enjoy overt displays of any kind.

"For half an hour, I guess," I say. "But I've booked the horse for four hours, in case of any equestrian delays—"

The doorbell rings, interrupting Paru's giggles.

Chako and Pinky arrive soon after the food. They've flown in from California. Both look sharp in jeans and fitted leather jackets—definitely a Pinky influence. Chako wasn't one to care about appearances when we did our undergrad together back in India. He is built for weddings, with nifty, easy-to-learn steps at his disposal, encouraging the stiffest people onto the dance floor. I'm glad he's here.

I take their jackets and suitcases to the guest room.

"Where's Samantha?" Chako asks, grabbing a paper plate and sitting on the floor around the coffee table. He opens the takeout boxes and we inhale the aroma of coconut and basil.

"Samantha's at her parents' place," I say.

"Oh, yeah?" Chako says. "Because your dad's here?"

"Yeah," I say. "It would be a major drama if he knew."

Pinky leans forward. "Wait, he doesn't know you guys live together?"

"Of course not! I'd get my butt kicked."

"So she moved out?" Pinky asks, incredulous.

"Yeah, packed her suitcases and removed all traces of her presence," I say.

"Wow, only to come back a few days later?"

"It's just easier, Pinky," I say.

"See, this is the problem with you guys," Pinky declares, placing her plate on the coffee table and using her hands to talk. "Look at me," she says, pointing at herself. "I'm almost forty, dating a guy five years younger than me, and I have no problem telling anyone that we live together."

Pinky is fun to be around, but she has a tendency to make everything about herself.

"Don't you think your dad would understand if you explained it to him?" she asks me.

I avoid making eye contact with Pinky. Chako looks like he's checked out of this conversation.

Paru says, "No way he'll understand. You know how Indian dads are." She eats a spoonful of red curry and says, "Goodness, this is spicy! But good, so good."

"And Samantha is okay with it?"

"Come on, Pinky, let it go," Chako says. "Samantha's going to be back in a couple of days. I'm sure she can stay away from her *fiancé* that long."

"But it's not about that, right?" Pinky says. "It's about tolerating these archaic ideas. And if you tolerate them, you are in fact propagating them."

"Pinky," Paru says, "Appa is progressive compared to many Indian parents. Samantha is half white and he's okay with that." She pauses, then goes on, "My mother-in-law—" she glances quickly out the window—"she used to visit us every year. She's great, bless her heart, but she's living in the nineteenth century. She had all these rules. She wouldn't let me enter the kitchen when I was on my period."

Pinky's face distorts in disbelief, her shoulders scrunching up to make clavicle depressions.

"In my own house!" Paru says. "She wouldn't let me touch the utensils. She'd give me food on a separate plate and purify her hands after that."

"What did your husband do about it?"

"Well, what could he do? He used to say she didn't mean any harm, which I get. But it was so annoying. She's had some health issues recently, so she hasn't visited for a few years. I'm scared that if my father-in-law passes away, she might move in with us."

"That is messed up," Pinky says. "Why can't you have a conversation with her directly?"

"And say what? That her entire life, everything she's believed in all these years, is nonsense and she has to change her outlook now?"

"At least when it comes to you and your life, yes."

"And do you think people change in their late sixties?" Paru says.

"That's what I'm saying. We *need* to have these uncomfortable conversations if we want things to change. Or else we'll continue these cycles. Just look at me, living my best life. Why do you think that's the case?"

"Do you have these conversations with your parents?" Paru asks, her nose crinkled up, which I know means she's really annoyed.

"Yes, I did! And they have pretty much disowned me because I speak my mind and refuse to get married to someone they find for me," Pinky says. "But I am true to myself, and that's why I'm happy."

No one says anything.

I am so relieved when the front door opens and my father, my brother-in-law, and my nephew walk in. My father smiles at Chako and Pinky. *Would* he understand? Our mother used to be the centre of our family, the place where conversation and tenderness flowed easily, now replaced by a hollow space, lumpy and jagged.

Chako gets up and says, "Hello, Uncle."

"When did you come?" my father asks.

"Just half an hour."

"You've put on weight."

Chako chuckles and says, "Uncle, this is Pinky."

"Your wife?"

Chako nods.

Pinky says, "No, Uncle, we're not married. We live together."

How easy to be this frank when it is not your own father.

Chako's face reddens. Paru tries to distract my father. "Appa, come to the dining table. I'll serve you lunch."

"Oh, live-in," my father says. "Yeah, it's common in India also these days. It's a good idea. Get to know each other better."

Paru and I look at each other, horrified.

Chako breaks into an uncomfortable laugh.

Pinky says, "You're absolutely right, Uncle," and looks at Paru, who runs into the kitchen.

My father slips into the kitchen to wash his hands and

returns, sitting down at the dining table. Paru transfers the food from the takeout boxes into bowls.

"What's in this?" my father asks.

"It's Thai curry," Paru says, putting some on his plate. "Chicken and vegetables in coconut milk. And mango salad."

"What's the green leaves?"

"Basil. The coconut milk is so thick—what do you think?"

He tastes it and says, "Not that fresh."

Paru sighs audibly. She is less patient with our father these days. I think it is because she is a mother—her patience is spent daily on other things.

"The mango is not ripe," he says, frowning.

"It's usually sweeter," I say. "Should I order something else for you, Appa?"

"No, no. This is fine. Better than pisa."

Alone at the table, he makes a well in the mound of rice on his plate and pours red curry into it. He mixes it and eats in silence. The afternoon sun, fragmented by the balcony railings, falls on my father in golden bands.

A Thing with Many Legs

I SLIP MY HAND inside my panties and close my eyes. This is the only way I can get out of bed these days. I think of Raji, imagining her naked body between my legs, and I come quickly.

It is the third morning I have woken up to no response from Raji, my phone's screen burnishing the pitch black of winter. I reread the last email she sent me—work-related—trying to read between the lines, mining for meaning, for a sign of something out of the ordinary. Something cumbersome, unwanted, has settled inside me, just above my chest. A thing with many legs crawling up my throat.

My boss, James, has called several times already. His last email read: *Where is the GREAT Raji? We go live in 24 hours!*

I refresh my inbox as I sit on the toilet and again as I brush my teeth. Months of toothpaste spray has built up along the edge of the mirror, and my reflection is spotty and dreadful, my stomach an unshapely bulge. One year is all it took. I swallow some toothpaste. Extreme Mint. Out of habit, I look at the top right corner of the bathroom. The slight spider is still there, its translucent body hanging by its silky web. It has been there for months, and it seems unreasonable to get rid of it now.

When I call James, he spits into the phone: "Tell me you know what is going on."

I was hired a year ago, straight out of university, to work in the IT department of a grocery chain in the Bay Area. I have worked from home nearly the entire year. Business is booming, so to speak—we are one of the few essential services still open. There is a go-live every few weeks when we launch a new application for the stores after rigorous testing by our offshore team in Bangalore.

"I'm trying to get hold of Raji," I say in a voice you would use to calm down a toddler.

James is swallowing his words again: "I don't understand you have worked with her attached at the hip for the last year you don't know where she is? And why was I told about this only yesterday?"

I mute myself and use the special words I have reserved for him, letting them out into the air bit by bit, releasing what is dark inside me.

When he pauses, I say, "It's unlike her not to respond to emails for days."

"I'm contacting the offshore vice-president," he says.

"Please give me a couple of hours," I plead. "She could lose her job."

"And you don't think this go-live is important enough?"

"I'll get hold of Raji, or I'll get Sai or Rajesh to do the work."

"We have to go up the ladder, not down, Mohak," James says. He says "Mohawk" with a confidence that would convince my own father that it is the correct way to pronounce my name.

In meetings, Raji and I are usually the only ones with our cameras turned on. Two weary faces in a sea of initials. She, a soft thing, with her pastel kurtas and freshly washed hair. Me, neglected potential, with my untidy bangs and fading sweatshirts. Raji never wears makeup aside from the thick kajal lining her eyes. Her lips are a dark brown and when she smiles, her eyes leap. She has a small black dot in the white of her right eye. A beauty spot, my mother would have said.

Raji works from the spare bedroom of her seventh-floor Bangalore apartment, unless her Wi-Fi is particularly choppy, in which case she risks going into the office. A wall of built-in cupboards and a long mirror is her background. From that room, she manages an all-male team of fifteen software developers and testers. My role is that of a business liaison, or a glorified messenger, as I like to think.

I try Raji's personal cellphone number, which she gave me months ago so we could text and it wouldn't show online in the office messenger. When she doesn't pick up, I worry it has something to do with her son, who has asthma.

My phone flashes—it is James. "Tell me this: You had the hand-off call, didn't you?" He says "hand-off" like he coined the expression.

"Sorry, James, it was a small code change, so I just emailed Raji," I say.

"Goodness, Mohak. Small code change? Do you realize the potential loss in revenue if shoppers don't get points as advertised?"

He genuinely believes this matter is of the utmost significance. Earth-shattering. He thinks he is equal to the front-line workers, saving lives by ensuring shoppers get loyalty points. He says he is hard on me because he is "grooming" me for a promotion.

"I meant the actual change in code is minor, not the business impact," I say, with practised patience.

"This is the problem with you people," he retorts.

With James, "you people" could mean any number of things. Here, it is people who don't get bonuses based on company revenue. The virus is continuing to make James richer.

I try to figure out the code myself. I see Raji all over it. The visually appealing indentation. The consistent naming of classes. Her signature comments that explain what each block of code does. Everything I know about the applications in this place, she has taught me.

Two years into my computer science degree, I realized I had no interest in it. It was my mother's plan; both her nieces had studied computer engineering back in India. I worked up the nerve to tell my mother that I wanted to switch majors, study photography maybe, and it didn't go well. Later, when she found out I was seeing a woman, she said I would be the death of her, blaming herself for giving me a boy's name. I ended the relationship. Soon after this, she was diagnosed with bone marrow cancer. On one of her worst days, she claimed she got the cancer because of all the shame I had caused her.

"Now I can't even die in peace," she said.

She died quickly. Painlessly, as they like to say in my family.

After that, I didn't bring up my lukewarm feelings toward my degree. Or date a woman. Imagine how selfish that would have been.

. . .

And now, Raji. About six months ago she was sitting at her desk, and the sun streaming through the window made her face turn an uncommon shade of orange and made me feel something infinite. In that moment, it seemed like we, as in the two of us, and we, as in all of us in this world living through these dreadful times, were going to be fine. More than fine—content, joyful, even with a bit of grace. It was one of those rare moments when you feel a connection with the rest of the world because this one person is giving you all their attention.

She was wearing a bright green kurta—parrot green, my mother would have called it—and I said, "You look beautiful in that kurta."

Her eyes on my screen grew wide, and her lips parted like she was saying something too big for words. Then I heard her say, "I got it recently. I love it so much," and she smiled like we both knew she wasn't talking about the kurta.

We skirted around whatever we were feeling in that moment until I asked her, "Have you ever been with a woman?"

And she said, "No!" and then she told me about her husband, who was away in the US for work, and I said, "Nice," and we started talking about work, and that was it.

. . .

James calls again around lunchtime. I have no update for him, so I ignore the call and try to think of an excuse. My mind wanders, imagining how it would feel to be someplace else. When Raji and I first started talking, I used to tell her I would visit Bangalore as soon as things got back to normal, and now it seems like such a cheap thing to say.

My father brings me up my lunch, panting a little. "Swarna Aunty got Covid," he says as he places the bowl of Instant Pot khichdi on my desk. "Girish Uncle must have it, too, but they're not testing in India now unless the symptoms are severe."

He is so earnest, I don't have the heart to tell him I have no idea who Swarna Aunty or Girish Uncle are, so I say, "That's so sad" and turn back to my laptop.

"It's pathetic. Hospitals don't have oxygen cylinders to keep people alive. You have to bring your own. The prime minister is more interested in Kumbh Mela and election campaigning," he says. "Amit can't even go see them because the borders are closed."

Amit must be the son. "Where is he?" I ask, turning to give him my attention. He is making my bed, folding my quilt into a rectangle instead of spreading it on the bed.

"Texas! You forgot?" he says, his nose twitching.

"I mean, I didn't know he was still there," I lie.

James calls again, and I show the phone to my father, mouthing *Boss*. He picks up my coffee mug and cereal bowl from the morning and leaves the room, closing the door behind him.

"So?" James says when I pick up.

"I'm working on the code myself," I say.

"Where the hell is Raji?"

"There must be some kind of emergency."

"What kind of a professional disappears like this with no backup days before a go-live?"

I mute myself and say the two special words.

"I'm emailing Srinivas," he says, referring to the vice-president of the Bangalore office. "These offshore people don't realize what we are. They're not grateful for the opportunity to work at a place like this, to get this kind of experience. We're retail gold! They just sit there and treat it like a nine-to-five job. None of them understand the business impact."

Listening to him talk like this, I feel that thing stuck in my throat come up. "Raji understands the business impact," I say, mentally waving goodbye to my upcoming promotion. "Despite how little difference it makes to her, especially now."

He hangs up on me.

• • •

For the past four months or so, Raji has been the only person I speak to every day. She started calling me outside of office hours soon after we began working together—it felt like such a normal thing to do then, to connect to another human being when we were stuck in our homes. She would call me on weekends while making tea. I'd say, "Good morning," and she'd say, "Good evening, how was your day?" She'd be in her kitchen, grating ginger, crushing cardamom, boiling tea leaves. The conversation was easy. She was good at picking up topic after topic, and I was good at listening. She'd tell me things she didn't tell anyone else, like how she was born in Canada and moved to India when she was eight because her mother needed a kidney transplant; how her aunt died in a train crash and her mother got her sister's kidneys; how her parents decided to stay in India to raise her aunt's kids, which gave her proxy siblings overnight; how she married someone she didn't love because she felt sorry for her mother, who badly wanted her to get married. Raji's only eight years older than me, but it seems like she has lived many lives. When I told her my mother had died, she told me how lucky we were to have found each other in the middle of all that darkness.

One evening, I'd drunk a couple of beers and had a nice feeling going, and I told her I loved her.

"I know," she said. "I love you, too."

After that, we never had to say it, because we knew it. We would watch movies together; I'd set everything up so we could watch the same movie at the same time and see each other on video. We would hold on to each other with our gaze and know that this was everything we wanted, even though we could never have it.

By late evening, I am done coding. I simply had to change the data type of a variable so the appropriate section of the code wouldn't be bypassed. I get someone to test it for me.

Meanwhile, James has emailed the vice-president in Bangalore and cc'd me.

Hi Srinivas—

We haven't heard from the team lead assigned to this weekend's go-live. She has been unavailable for three days without arranging for a backup, giving no intimation of her whereabouts. We have absorbed the responsibility for this go-live, and it will be delivered entirely from here. I would like a proper replacement immediately.

—James

He writes "team lead," like Raji doesn't have a name. For the past year, he has made money and a reputation out of the work that Raji did, and now she is just a title.

The thought that I won't get to work with Raji any longer gets hold of me in an unkind way. I wonder if we can continue whatever we have even if we don't have work to keep us together.

When Raji doesn't call me on Friday night—her Saturday morning—I begin to pray for the first time since my mother died.

The go-live on Saturday runs smoothly. Shoppers get points as advertised in the flyer. Some stores make record sales.

On Sunday morning an email creeps into my inbox and stays there for four hours before I see it. I read it on my phone as I brush my teeth. I read it again, sitting on the edge of the bathtub. I stare at the ceiling, and at the spider, and I read it again, picking the wound, hoping it will hurt less.

Dear James,

On behalf of the Bangalore office, I apologize for the lack of support for the weekend go-live. It was an unprecedented situation. Raji Srinivasan, the lead assigned to the project, contracted covid-19 and passed away in less than 24 hours. We have assigned a new lead, Chaitanya Kumar, to the project. He is a manager and has worked in retail for over 10 years. I have copied him on this email. I will let Chaitanya get in touch with your team.

Sincerely,

Srinivas Iyer

I cannot find a way to hold this knowledge inside me. I think about deleting the email, going back to a time when it hadn't been written, but this image pops into my head: Raji in her parrot-green kurta, gasping for air, waiting at the hospital with no one to attend to her. Oxygen cylinder is the currency, and Raji isn't wealthy enough.

James sends me a blank email with the subject: *Set up a meeting with Chaitanya ASAP.*

I call James.

"That was a lot!" he says, still refusing to say her name.

"You know Raji risked her life to go to the office last week because her Wi-Fi at home was spotty. For *this* job."

"It's sad, I know, but it is what it is." He pauses. "Start the knowledge transfer with this new—"

I hang up on him.

Of all the three million people who died last year, not one of them stirred anything in me. And now, all the hurt, everything that is unjust, hits me at once. I feel like I am choking, as if I am the one who can't hack air into my lungs. I need to do something to stop feeling what I am feeling. An idea gets hold of me.

The logic is simple. For every product in the flyer, change the product name that will be printed on the bill. I have to jump through a few hoops to send the code to the stores, but I manage to get approval because I lie about what the code is doing.

The next morning, the CEO wants answers. He needs to issue a press release.

Before they fix it, I go to the store nearest to me. I want to see it happening. I dump a bunch of things into my cart, remembering the items in the flyer. Toilet paper, 1,500 points. Fabric softener, 500 points. Pack of ginger ale, 700 points. I use the self-checkout.

My heart is pounding as the bill prints. It is long and crisp and flowy. Three items on the bill and a poem of points. The prices are correct, and so are the points, but the item descriptions are all the same:

WE DON'T CARE ABOUT HUMAN LIVES

By the time they trace it back to me, James will have lost his job, or at least his credibility. And I will be long gone.

For now, I go home and lock myself in the bathroom. The spider has gone, leaving behind a hollow web. I get in the shower, soaking my T-shirt and jeans, and let out the tears, that thing now lodged in my throat. The heaviness, the heaving, this utter loneliness.

Rahel

SHE WORE AN OLIVE-GREEN TURTLENECK and black pants, her thick curly hair threatening to escape the tight bun it was packed into, her skin the texture of plums, and her eyes the colour of Alappuzha backwaters. Her name—Rahel Varghese—was displayed on a tag pinned over her left breast. No makeup, not even lipstick, nail colour peeling, loose-fitting clothes that didn't give a hint as to what was underneath—she had a freeness about her that came from not caring about her looks. She sat easily on the leather chair like a man, not bothering to cross her legs or lean forward delicately.

"I remember you," she said, grinning, between sips of Pepsi. "You used to have a moustache back then."

"What self-respecting Malayali didn't have a moustache back then?" Freddie said, not wanting to admit he had no memory of her.

Her laugh was husky, full-throated. It had the quality of being both ridiculous and the only way to laugh.

Freddie had never noticed Rahel back in college in Kochi. Their paths may have crossed a few times in the grand hallways or massive examination rooms, but he did not remember her sparking any interest in him until that afternoon fifteen years later, during lunch at the convention centre in Toronto. He learned about her through his wife, who was a distant relative of hers. He tracked her down easily, as she was the only other Indian engineer there.

"So, how long have you been in Johannesburg?" she asked.

"Last seven years." Freddie leaned in. "I started out in Delhi after college, in a small construction company. Then I got this offer in South Africa from one of its largest mining companies. And I've been there ever since. I'm a senior engineer now. On track to become staff engineer next year."

This type of self-promotion came easily to Freddie, but Rahel seemed unimpressed. She smiled the way you do when you have to tolerate someone at your workplace. She ate the catered lunch fast, glancing at her watch often.

Afterward, she lit a cigarette and offered one to Freddie.

Freddie refused, unable to hide the disdain on his face.

She didn't seem to notice, or perhaps she didn't care. She relaxed back into her chair and said, "I've never been to South Africa."

"One of the most incredible countries I've ever been to,"

Freddie said. "And I've been to more than thirty countries. The political climate is a shame, though."

"So you travel a lot?"

"Nature of my work," he said.

Rahel leaned forward on the table, resting her chin on her interlaced fingers. "Tell me about Johannesburg."

"Johannesburg is great, but Cape Town is the place to be. The most beautiful place in the world. Mountains and oceans, whatever you want," Freddie said.

"We should go there sometime then," she said, not blinking.

"We should," Freddie said. *What a strange woman*, he thought. Unladylike and forward. Probably one of those bra-burning feminists—perhaps not bra burning, for he could see the outline of a strap.

"I shall take you to my favourite place in Toronto," she said. "If you want," she added, seeing the surprise in his eyes.

"I would love that," he said finally.

They agreed to meet outside Rahel's house at six the next morning, a Sunday. She lived in a brick-faced semi-detached house near Trinity Bellwoods, that sprawling park in the heart of the city.

This was the mid-eighties, but there was none of the big hair, big shoulders, oversized jackets for Rahel. She was apathetic about fashion. She wore another long-sleeved, dark turtleneck, paired with beige Bermuda shorts. Around her waist, a purple fanny pack. Freddie had swapped his business suit for an oversized white blazer with large shoulder pads, khakis, and an expensive pair of loafers his wife had given him for his thirtieth birthday. He hadn't spoken to his wife since he'd arrived in Toronto and didn't intend to tell her about this day trip.

Now, Freddie had had many lovers, but Rahel was not the type of woman he usually pursued. Although he was only an inch taller than Rahel, who stood about five-foot-two, Freddie went for tall women with large derrières. He had the confidence, and he knew what he wanted: to hold up their arses and sink his face into them.

As they walked to the subway station, Freddie asked Rahel if she lived with someone.

She said, "Living alone since seventy-eight. Divorced after a year of marriage." And then offered the explanation that her husband had left when he found out they couldn't have kids.

"That's too bad," Freddie said, now grasping why Rahel was the way she was. She had no reason to prove anything to anyone.

"It's not too bad, if you think about it," she said. "I'm quite happy."

"You have a great house," Freddie said, in lieu of an apology.

His own marriage was a business deal. Both his and his wife's parents were in the gold business, and both families would profit from the union. The wedding had been front-page news in Kerala. Two rivals coming together to monopolize the sale of gold jewellery in the state. The one thing in Kerala apart from coconuts that always had a market.

Rahel retrieved a worn-out city map from her fanny pack and explained the route to Freddie. "In case we get separated," she said.

"I don't intend to get separated from you," he said, observing the shape of her lips.

First, they embarked on the ferry that would take them to the Toronto Islands. To Freddie, Lake Ontario looked vapid in comparison to the Atlantic and Indian Oceans surrounding Cape Town, yet Rahel's enthusiasm was enormous.

When they were halfway between the city and the island, Rahel led Freddie to the edge of the boat. The water had taken on the colour of the sun, a shimmering gold. "This is why I wanted to start so early," she said.

The ferry cut through the morning, ushering the cool air from the water into the boat, and Rahel crossed her arms, hunching her body into a ball. Freddie offered her his blazer, but she said, "I'm not a delicate darling."

When they arrived on the island, Rahel stepped to the side and started doing lunges. One leg forward, one backward—and bend. Freddie looked at her, bewildered, and she explained, "Lunges make you warmer."

People stared at them as Rahel lunged on one leg, then the other. Freddie laughed until his cheeks hurt.

They began to walk, passing a park where teenagers in bikinis rode a miniature train, and a pond where little kids in sunhats rode in giant white swan boats.

Rahel said, "Here, there's a shortcut."

They cut across a large lawn and the chatter of the kids faded. They entered a wooded area, then Rahel led Freddie through the trees to a small clearing that overlooked the lake, the city. Across the lake was the Toronto skyline, the needle of the CN Tower holding up the clouds. Tall maples shaded the clearing, making it feel like a well-kept secret.

"This," Rahel said, "is my favourite spot."

Before Freddie could respond, she said, "Sit here," pointing to a spot on the grass.

Freddie did as instructed, and Rahel sat down beside him. "I've never been here with anyone else before," she said, as if this realization had just come to her.

"Me neither," Freddie said.

A chuckle escaped him, and she laughed that laugh of hers again.

From South Africa letters arrived for Rahel once a week, sometimes twice. For an engineer, Freddie's writing was ornate and elaborate. He wrote that he had remembered

Rahel from college but was too shy to tell her in person in Toronto because he'd had a crush on her back then. This Rahel found simply improbable—she could always tell if someone liked her—but it felt nice coming from Freddie. Rahel was too shy to respond to these confessions, so she reported on the weather and her new job as lead engineer at a manufacturing plant. She reserved her early mornings to write to him, filling up pages every day and mailing them the following Monday.

She always ended her letters by asking him how he was feeling. To which he responded by describing, in great detail, the emptiness that surrounded him:

> *Today was one of those days when everything makes you sad. The way raindrops fall on the windshield. The mound of topsoil in a pickup truck. The way the road bends and dips. The way your shoulders put up with a thousand little injustices.*
>
> *When I reached home after work, she had already left for some party or other with her boyfriend. The nanny had already put the kids to bed. I made myself an egg sandwich, and now I am sitting down and writing to you. Thinking about you, your faultless mind, makes me feel at peace.*
>
> *When, dear, can I see you again?*

Rahel's writing was less poetic—she stuck to simple language, facts. She wrote about her boss and her responsibilities at work. Her boss had three kids, so he left at 3 p.m. every day to pick them up, leaving Rahel in charge.

She learned about Freddie's peculiar marital arrangement. That his family was worth millions, but he didn't want any of it. That he had refused to join the family business and had paved his own path. That his wife was way out of his league and reminded him of it often. That she brought her boyfriend home when Freddie was away for work. Rahel felt a strange satisfaction when she read this, but she wrote back that she was sorry he was unhappy.

He replied that "one's circumstances have little to do with the degree of one's happiness."

Freddie's letters were from another dimension. They helped Rahel get out of her rut, let her organized brain wander.

He wrote:

You have to grab joy where you find it.

Do you have things you want to do before you die? A list of sorts?

I was indulging in such an exercise on my drive to Cape Town yesterday, and it may interest you that you appeared in nearly all the items on my list. What is happening to me, my love?

1. Take Rahel to Cape Town.

2. Make love to Rahel in every country in the world.

3. Live in a small bungalow with a front porch and a rose garden with Rahel.

4. Raise my beautiful children with Rahel by my side.

5. Learn carpentry and make things with my hands.

What would be on your list?

Rahel had never received such a letter from anyone. Freddie made her feel things she didn't remember feeling in a long time. Certainly not since she got married, and divorced. Perhaps in high school, for a boy who left pavizhamalli flowers—white, with orange centres—on her desk in the shape of a heart.

Like misremembered lyrics, a young, moustachioed Freddie began to appear in her memories. Once, on the college bus, he stood beside her and told her that a business rival had planted a spy in his father's office. It led to a major financial loss, and his father suffered a cardiac arrest as a result. Freddie had appeared so disturbed that Rahel went looking for him the next day in the chemical engineering building at the other end of campus. Freddie told her that he had never experienced such kindness.

Regret settled in Rahel's body for not loving Freddie when she had the chance.

Are you serious? she replied. *If so, I will send my list.*

• • •

Three months passed, and Freddie flew back to Toronto. He had convinced his boss that he needed to oversee an investment the company had made in person. He surprised Rahel outside her office, and she invited him home for dinner.

Rahel cooked egg fried rice while Freddie sat at the kitchen counter and told her about his travels. He talked about his coin collection—folders and folders of coins displayed under clear plastic—from the thirty-plus countries he had visited.

Rahel was unlike any of the other women Freddie had slept with. He liked how quickly she got turned on and how non-performative the whole thing was. Her eyes never left his.

She told him she hadn't been with anyone in years. Not since her divorce almost ten years ago.

"What a shame," Freddie said, "for you are so good in bed."

Rahel climbed over him and rubbed him with her body, as if to provide further proof. She held the back of his head like a precious artifact.

They managed to meet only twice or sometimes thrice a year. Always in Toronto, although Freddie still talked about taking Rahel to Cape Town. Freddie was promoted to staff engineer and, shortly afterward, engineering manager.

Rahel felt the weight of that responsibility on their relationship. His letters became shorter and less poetic. Still, he wrote to her almost every week. He talked more about his kids, who, as they got older, ignored him more than ever.

"It is easy to be forgotten," he told Rahel on the phone.

"I would never forget you," Rahel said, cringing as the words left her mouth. "I don't mean to make it a competition," she added.

Rahel was a Canadian citizen by then and could travel more easily to South Africa. Freddie booked a room in a new luxury hotel overlooking Table Mountain on one side and the Atlantic Ocean on the other. Rahel shaved her legs and bought new bathing suits for the trip. Freddie didn't leave her side, except to phone his kids twice a day. He held her hand as they strolled on the beach, sat in restaurants, walked by peace protests. He commented on little things about her, things that no one else had ever noticed. The small scar on her forehead from when she had fallen as a five-year-old. The light birthmark on the side of her right calf. The way her spine dipped and arched.

On Rahel's last night in Cape Town, she blurted out the questions she had managed not to ask during their years together.

They had just made love. "It's breaking my heart to leave now," she said, holding Freddie in a tight embrace, looking up at him, her chin resting on his chest. "Don't you love me?

Why would you want to spend the rest of your life with someone you don't love?"

Rahel expected him to say he was staying because of the kids, but he said, "It's the family business, you know that." He tried to escape from her arms.

"But you're not in the business, right?"

"It's not whether I'm involved in the business or not. I am the sole heir to all the family wealth." He sounded tired, as if it were exhausting to explain this to her. "If I leave the marriage, I get no inheritance."

Rahel released Freddie and sat up on the edge of the bed. She stared at the pattern on the carpet: black hexagons surrounded by bright chaos. "But I thought you didn't care about the money," she said.

"If you knew how many zeros are in the number, you would care about it, too."

When Rahel returned to Toronto, she received a telegram from Freddie:

Do not write. Wife found out about us. I will contact you when things settle.

Was this the end? Like the smell of an evening campfire, Freddie had seeped into every nook of Rahel's body. Not the Freddie who had emerged on the last night of her trip, but the Freddie who could have been hers.

Life disappeared from Rahel's house. She stood in each doorway, examining the rooms as if she had just moved into a strange new hotel miles away from home. She began to spend long hours at the plant, dreading to return to the place where the loss of her love was most apparent.

The manufacturing plant was a long building with a row of equidistant square windows on the side facing the road. At sundown, when she left the plant, they looked like orange Post-it notes, each one a reminder of a task left undone.

Rahel immersed herself in her job. She began to do her boss's work, too, relieving him of most of his responsibilities. She did not ask for a pay raise, and he did not offer one. She was supervising a team of men, who treated her differently because she was a woman. They laid their inconveniences on her, calling in sick at the last minute or demanding more time to finish their work.

Three months after the telegram, a postcard arrived from Freddie. It was from Amsterdam, where he was staying for business. It read:

Work has been terribly busy.
How are you, my love?
Wish you were here with me.

Rahel replied to the address in Amsterdam, not knowing how long he would be there. She told him she had been worried all these months. Freddie wrote back quickly, not addressing her concerns. He explained that he was now in charge of all his company's European operations. Rahel had many questions—the nature of his work confused her—but she chose to save them for their next meeting.

Which was the following year, back in Cape Town. They carried on as before; Rahel asked no questions about his wife and Freddie offered no information.

Rahel's trips to Cape Town became her yearly vacations, her time away from her boss and her work and her home. Freddie visited Toronto, too. He had a key to Rahel's house and would let himself in when he arrived. Sometimes he surprised Rahel, but she preferred it when he gave her notice. This way she could shave her legs beforehand.

Freddie was gentle in bed, and it was easy for them to satisfy each other. Rahel often commented how easy it was for them to make love, how their bodies fit together perfectly. She didn't have much control over Freddie, but she didn't want to do anything that would make him want to stop.

Freddie was an only child. As far back as he could remember, his family had had expectations of him. Expectations that he would run the business his grandfather had built and his father grew. When Freddie decided to build a career of his own, as far away from his family as possible, his parents regretted not having more kids. They were thrilled when Freddie's wife quickly produced two children—a boy and a girl—and told themselves and anyone who would listen that ambition and excellence sometimes skip a generation.

Freddie wasn't even sure the children were his. Neither of them resembled him, but they didn't look like their mother either. Freddie didn't lack ambition; he just knew himself well enough to know he wouldn't be happy rooted in one place. He needed constant change, stimulation, women, romance, secrecy, in order to be happy. His marriage was a good arrangement. If his wife had expected fidelity, life would have been hard.

Freddie had no use for guilt. He told his trusted secretary, Zola, who sent his letters to his different lovers, that, like Márquez, his heart had more rooms than a whorehouse. When he was with a woman, he was with her fully, he loved her completely, so in that sense his affairs were never a betrayal.

Usually, Freddie didn't care to keep a woman who demanded too much from him. But he couldn't let go of Rahel. He had tried—he stayed away for months after sending the telegram lying about his wife finding out about them. He had done this to loosen Rahel's grip, to prevent her from becoming too clingy, the way some women do. But he could feel her love across the oceans, always there, dripping, overflowing. She loved him like a parent, expecting nothing in return. And she had no one else. She wasn't like him—able to find love anywhere. She was the kind who could love only one person in a lifetime.

Eventually, Freddie's wife did find out about one of his lovers: Sophie from Amsterdam. Sophie was fifteen years younger, a lean-limbed blonde with insatiable desire. It played out almost exactly like the fiction Freddie had spun for Rahel in the telegram he'd sent her all those years ago. By now, his wife had grown disillusioned with their arrangement. She was nearing forty and had broken up with her long-term boyfriend. She was becoming increasingly difficult to live with. The things that used to distract her—status, wealth, her appearance, the promise of stability—were shifting. A new South Africa was emerging, and freedom was on everyone's mind.

She found pictures of Sophie one day when she showed up at Freddie's office, unannounced. If they had been pictures of Rahel, she probably wouldn't have cared—Rahel's plain face and drab clothes would not have provoked her. But Sophie and her youth brought out a madness in her. She phoned her parents and Freddie's parents in India and made a big deal about the affair. The two sets of parents called a family meeting. Freddie and his wife left for Kerala, leaving the kids with the nanny in Johannesburg.

Freddie and his wife stayed in his parents' big house in

Alappuzha for months while the family tried to force them to repair their relationship.

"I would like a divorce," Freddie said, suddenly missing Rahel terribly. "I can't live like this anymore."

"Die-vorce?" his father said. "You will die before you die-vorce." And he grounded Freddie as though he were a teenager.

His mother showed him some mercy, but she, like everyone in his father's life, was merely an accessory.

Freddie's wife made a big scene, claiming she was stuck in a loveless marriage, playing the long-suffering wife flawlessly. Freddie didn't complain, didn't bring up her infidelities—he would be blamed for these as well.

Things cooled down when he proposed that they go on vacation to Venice for his wife's fortieth birthday. They stayed in a hotel overlooking a piazza for a week. Freddie forgave easily. Since he didn't hold attachments, he didn't hold grudges either.

When he got back to Johannesburg, he wrote to Sophie, describing how he missed the way she offered her bare arse to him. Sophie had done things in bed no one else had. He wasn't ready to lose that.

He also responded to the many letters from Rahel.

As he dropped his letters off on Zola's desk, she laughed, saying, "Getting right back on the horse, huh?"

"Cost me a trip to Venice."

"Peanuts for you," she drawled in her sexy Afrikaans accent Freddie loved.

Sophie didn't respond. She had probably moved on. What a shame. And he didn't hear from Rahel. It was unlike her not to write back. She always wrote back. She had no one else. His calls also went unanswered. Over nine months went by, and he made plans to go to Toronto. But the weekend before his departure, he got a call from his uncle. His mother had died in her sleep. The only member of his family who had treated him not just as the heir to millions but as a person with feelings.

The funeral was a weeklong affair. The coffin was polished teak with brass handles. His father wore a three-piece suit with a red satin pocket square. His eyes were moist and his nose was red, although Freddie knew that he wasn't mourning his wife but rather the loss of familiarity.

He called Rahel. He needed her then. Not his father or his wife or any of his other lovers. He was so relieved to hear her voice he broke into sobs.

He went to Rahel straight from the funeral. Told his wife it was an urgent business trip. Rahel held him as he wept after they made love. Freddie knew he was the greatest love of Rahel's life. Telling her she was the only one for him, that he couldn't be with anyone but her, was an act of kindness. He had to make her believe she was the greatest love of his life, too. For her to carry on, to live one day after another.

Freddie's job took him to Toronto often; at other times, he would fly Rahel to South Africa. To his relief, his wife had rekindled the affair with her old boyfriend and was off Freddie's back. He never had to worry about being seen with Rahel. In Toronto, no one knew him, and in Cape Town, no one knew either of them. Even if someone did see them together, they could easily be mistaken for siblings, or cousins. They were both short and had similar features—round faces, black hair, thick eyebrows.

Years passed in this way, and Freddie lost most of his other lovers. He was in his fifties now and losing the need for sex. Every now and then, when he wanted to prove to himself that he could still charm women, he would stir up something with a girl half his age. It wasn't difficult—he had the money and the power—but these affairs never lasted long. Freddie didn't want them to. They were simply sexual. Apart from his marriage, his relationship with Rahel was the longest he'd had.

The alumni group from Freddie and Rahel's college set up a reunion in Kochi. Freddie felt a nostalgia he had never experienced before. He emailed Rahel about the reunion, but she said she couldn't make it because she would be on a work trip to São Paulo. It was unlike her to miss an opportunity to be with him.

Freddie went anyway, and he missed Rahel more than he had imagined. Suddenly, all he wanted was to have her by his side, to listen to her solid, comforting voice. For people to see them together, an unlikely pair who had stood the test of time simply because they loved each other.

On a Tuesday six years later, Freddie received the call. The caller said that Rahel had named Freddie in her will. He received an email with details of the funeral. It included a recent headshot of Rahel—almost in profile wearing a blazer, her hair done, and her lips a dark maroon. There was no way this could be his Rahel. There was no way she was not breathing anymore, no way he wasn't occupying her mind anymore.

He flew to Toronto the next morning. The funeral was not as fancy as his mother's funeral in Alappuzha, but there were lots of fresh flowers. It was plain and solid, just like Rahel. The chapel was packed with faces he didn't recognize. Ghosts from a life he wasn't a part of. The sadness of everyone in the room floated through the air and concentrated around Freddie. There were hardly any dry eyes. Who were all these people?

Rahel had lost her parents a few years earlier, and like Freddie, she was an only child. It occurred to him how little he knew about her life aside from the part that included him. Over time, it seemed that she told him less and less about her life. There had been no other man, that he was sure of, but he realized that lately she had rarely spoken about her friends or how she spent her weekends. He hadn't asked, either. For years, she had accommodated his schedule, often sitting alone in a hotel room for hours waiting for him to get out of some meeting or other.

The top half of the casket was open, and Rahel lay there, her face looking so different, like that of a taxidermied animal. Freddie closed his eyes and saw Rahel. Rahel from the first time he visited Toronto, when she took him to Toronto Island, in a turtleneck and Bermuda shorts.

A woman who introduced herself as Kala Ramesh cried as she gave the eulogy, her bent nose twitching to the left every time she sniffled. He remembered her name from Rahel's letters from long ago, something about a friend who sold peacock accessories. She looked like she would have been attractive when she was younger—well dressed, bright lipstick, shapely brows. She wore a black lace dress and dangling earrings made of peacock feathers. She said she had met Rahel fifteen years ago at the community centre, where they took swimming lessons. Rahel was the one person she had looked up to consistently, she said. "She had a flair for life that was contagious. She knew how to live on her own terms. She was always learning something new—salsa, pottery, carpentry. Her home was full of the beautiful things she made." Freddie thought about the little ceramics he had seen in Rahel's house. He had never asked where they came from. "Not only was she an inspiring and decorated engineer, she was also a magnanimous human being who made friends wherever she went. She knew how to love people, and she knew how to love herself."

If not for the images of Rahel displayed in the slide show on the TV, Freddie would have thought Kala was talking about a different person. He had not seen any of these pictures. He recognized some of Rahel's clothes, even a dress he had bought for her in Paris, but he didn't recognize the way Rahel carried herself.

"Thank you for coming," Kala said to Freddie when he introduced himself to her. "I'm sure it would have meant a lot to Rahel."

Freddie was irritated by the way she talked as if she knew Rahel better than he did. "I've known Rahel since we were teenagers," he said. "How did this happen?"

"She was diagnosed a year ago, but we thought she would make it," Kala said. "This last decline was rapid and unexpected."

"What did you mean in the eulogy—I mean, when you said she lived life on her own terms?" Freddie asked.

"Well," Kala said, "I mean, she didn't have any grand self-righteous ideas about right and wrong or how one should be. She was just who she was, all the time. She loved people with abandon, but she also knew clearly what she wanted for herself."

"Was she happy?"

"Happier than most people I know. She suffered great

heartbreak with her husband, and then another guy broke her heart terribly many years ago. That was a big blow for her. It took her months to recover. But afterward, she changed a lot. For the better, if you ask me. She couldn't be bothered to find someone steady, get married, and do that dance again. She wanted to live alone, but she was in no way alone," she said, her eyes brightening.

"What do you mean?" Freddie said.

"She had many lovers. A lover in Cape Town. One in São Paolo. Another in London, or rather, one with whom she went to London. One in New York."

Freddie looked at her with hurt eyes, as if every word she said was one too many for him to handle. "A lover in Cape Town," he said to himself.

At the office of Rahel's lawyer, Freddie found Kala again. She was in charge of selling Rahel's house and would get a portion of the profits. Freddie didn't recognize any name in the will except an orphanage in Kochi, which he vaguely remembered Rahel mentioning. She had amassed a considerable fortune for someone who did not start out wealthy. Most of the money would go to the orphanage. To Freddie, Rahel had willed an original painting from Thailand. What an odd thing to leave him, he thought. But then again, any money she could have left Freddie wouldn't have made a great difference to his wealth.

Freddie went to Rahel's house and tried his key. It still

worked. Inside, everything looked almost exactly as it had the last time he was there six months ago. He went into every room, as if hoping to find Rahel there. In the bedroom, he sat on the bed they had shared. Across from the bed was a tall dresser and above it hung the painting from Thailand.

Freddie wished so much to have Rahel back, if only for a few hours, to ask what Kala was talking about. Who were all those lovers? Why had she led him to believe he was the only one? Who had broken her heart so badly? He wished she were there to lie on his chest and tell him in her grounding voice that he was the only love of her life.

Freddie fell asleep on Rahel's bed, hugging the pillow that still smelled of her.

The sun streams through the curtains and wakes him.

Freddie looks out the window and sees that the trees are leafless in July.

He has found the answer. There's nothing to ask Rahel.

Zola, his secretary, was trustworthy but human. She had made a mistake. After Freddie and his wife returned from Venice, Zola had sent the letter intended for Sophie to Rahel. Something had changed in Rahel after that. She had become less needy, she asked less of him, which was what he wanted at the time.

How many decades has it taken him to figure this out?

Freddie stares at the painting in Rahel's bedroom, the one she left him in her will. A naked goddess is surrounded by many shirtless lovers. A gold necklace sits just above her bare breasts, and her eyes are lost in thought, or pleasure. The lovers, mesmerized, notice nothing but her.

Maths Club

DEVI VIJAYSHANKAR IS TEN when she moves to a boarding school in Trivandrum, leaving her parents, who have jobs in Saudi Arabia. It is her father's decision, for the sake of her education, and she gladly goes along with it. She has read enough Enid Blyton books set in charming, castle-like British boarding schools where the girls have a lifetime's worth of experiences and adventures to know that this separation from her parents will only lead to an exciting life. Growing up in a tiny desert town in Saudi Arabia, where nothing happens, Devi is eager for a new and exciting life.

It turns out that the boarding school residence Devi ends up in is as far from her imagination as possible—a beige box of a building the size of a three-storey house, dorm rooms stacked with bunk beds, and a warden with a large mole on her upper lip who watches the girls' every move and doesn't let them play or even hum a tune.

The school itself is somewhat decent, a U-shaped building with a rectangular courtyard at its centre. Devi's classroom is on the ground floor, and through its open doors she can see the wide corridor and the courtyard beyond it. The beginning of the school year coincides with the start of the monsoons, bringing the most incessant rains, which amazes Devi, coming from the desert. The classroom windows wear blue tarp curtains that lend a bluish tint to everything in those early months.

On the day Devi meets Nair Sir, the beloved maths teacher she's heard so much about, the rains have stopped. She sees Nair Sir outside her ninth-grade classroom, crouching in front of the stray dog that saunters into the corridor in the afternoons. He peels a banana and carefully removes its strings, while the dog waits, drool spilling over the edges of its mouth. He breaks the banana into small pieces and lets the dog eat out of his hand. Nair Sir has big hair, below his ears, and his shoulders are narrow, as if he needs to fit through spaces too small for him. When the bell rings, Devi's teacher, Miss Meenu, asks her to help bring the students' notebooks to the staff room. As they approach Nair Sir, he gets up and throws the banana peel under a tree in the courtyard. He pulls out a folded, faded checkered handkerchief from his back pocket and wipes his hands.

"You're encouraging the strays," Miss Meenu says, shaking her head. "And—do you walk around with bananas in your pocket every day?"

"You never know when you might need a banana," he says, laughing as if he has said something he shouldn't have. When he purses his lips to hold in his laugh, his clean-shaven upper lip stretches, giving it a green tinge. With no facial hair and a lean frame, he looks younger than the other male teachers—PT Sir, Art Sir, and Yoga Sir, all referred to by the subjects they teach like they are replaceable, but not Nair Sir.

"You're one of a kind," Miss Meenu says, one side of her lips turning down, her eyebrows raised. She's wearing a pink polyester saree, the loose end grazing the floor.

Nair Sir picks it up, saying, "You'll trip."

Miss Meenu quickly wraps the saree around her back and tucks it into her waist.

The dog hops by as they cross the courtyard, the August sun beating down, leaving sweat stains in plain sight—on Miss Meenu's blouse, on the back of Devi's shirt, and on the edge of Nair Sir's collar.

"See, now we can't get rid of the dog," Miss Meenu says.

Nair Sir picks up a stone, pretend-throws it at the dog, and it bounces away. "There. Happy?" he says.

In the staff room, Devi sees many of her teachers. They

look different here, leaning over their lunch boxes with playful eyes.

"So, is this the new student everyone is talking about?" Nair Sir asks, without looking at Devi.

"Yes, this is Devi," Miss Meenu says, as if showing off something that is not hers.

"I hear you're quite the superstar," Nair Sir says, and Devi focuses on arranging the notebooks neatly on Miss Meenu's desk, her ears tingling.

"So, your parents are in Dubai?" Nair Sir asks.

"In Saudi Arabia, sir."

"All that Saudi oil money," he says, rubbing his thumb and pointer finger together. "You must have a grand mansion in Kowdiar."

"No, we don't have a house here. I stay with my grandparents during the holidays."

"I run a maths club on Friday evenings from five to six. It's free, and you're welcome to join us."

A maths club?! Any club!

Devi's chemistry teacher interjects, "There he goes, recruiting the innocent ones."

"I don't understand how Nair has time for such things," Miss Meenu says.

What does she mean by "such things"? Something frivolous? Something extra?

"Where is it?" Devi asks.

"In the IIB classroom," Nair Sir says. "Come check it out tomorrow." He looks at Devi and tilts his head, as though considering her for an important job.

Devi's face flushes and she thinks perhaps this is how her adventures will begin.

Nair Sir dresses differently from the other teachers. In his cotton button-down shirts tucked into his blue jeans, he looks like one of the students. Out of the seven students in the club, all except for Devi are in the eleventh and twelfth grades. They are all too good-looking for a maths club. Jacob and Govind (who has a moustache!) are flirting with Tina, who looks like a model with her short bob and popped collar. How different the school uniform looks on Tina, so full of style. Ashwathy and Aishwarya (both Ash for short) are sitting together, giggling and factoring equations like a synchronized swim team. Jay is the tallest of them all, with high cheekbones and smooth hair that falls softly on his forehead—what he lacks in maths skills, he makes up for with his looks. And then there's Devi, with her flat chest and braids, the fledgling.

Devi is elated to be here. It's a welcome change from sitting alone in her dorm room, listening to music on her CD player, and writing down the lyrics in a notebook, waiting to practise them when the warden steps out to get her eyebrows done or go shopping. She has gotten good at "My Heart Will Go On." The movie *Titanic* has been all the rage for a few months, but she hasn't had the chance to see it yet. The poster of Leo and Kate with the ship is plastered on walls all over the city. Images from the film have found their way onto notebook covers and pencil cases and ballpoint pens. Her father always makes it a point to take Devi to the movies when they are in India, as cinemas are banned in Saudi Arabia. Devi loves the entire experience: the dim lighting, the fragrant popcorn, the massive screen—it feels like being part of something bigger than her small life.

Unlike in a traditional classroom, Nair Sir doesn't teach the entire group at the same time. The blackboard remains untouched. He gives out assignments and sits down with each student to make sure the concepts are understood. The more exercises they complete, the more he gives them. And instead of disciplining them when they talk, he joins their conversations.

"How's the new home?" he asks Tina.

"Smells like varnish," Tina says.

"When are you inviting us over?" Nair Sir wants to know.

"Do you need an invitation?" Tina says.

Govind says, "Yes, man, do you need an invitation?"

"I am your teacher, show some respect," Nair Sir says, and laughs. "We have a new student here!" he announces.

"She looks harmless," Govind says, eyeing Devi.

Devi squirms in her chair and pretends to be focused on her algebraic expressions.

"You forgot to simplify. Again!" Nair Sir says to Tina. He sits down beside her and shows her examples.

When he comes around to Devi, she has completed all the equations, eager to please. He checks them and says, "Fabulous! Look at this, guys. Devi on her first day—one hundred percent." He holds up her notebook and shows it to the other kids. "Gold star!"

"Great! There's a nerd among us," Jacob says.

Nair Sir shows Devi how to factorize using cross multiplication, which is much faster than the way her teacher taught her. It is after 6:30 p.m., but they all linger, chatting away. Devi has never been in a classroom this late. The desks and benches adopt a freer, friendlier disposition.

"We're going to stop by the Ganesh Bakery for puffs," Tina says to Devi. "You wanna come?"

Devi is surprised by the offer, coming from someone so beautiful and cool. Tina doesn't stay at the dorm like Devi but comes to school by bus. Devi had to get special permission from her warden just to attend maths club. The warden likes girls who are docile, who speak only when spoken to, the ones who get married early and devote themselves to their families. Devi's parents, and even her grandparents, simply want her to come back home before dark.

"We aren't allowed to leave the campus this late," Devi says.

Nair Sir's eyes turn dull. Devi wants to go with them and not worry about the warden, but she hasn't forgotten what happened to the girl who was caught with her boyfriend having ice cream at a café last month. The warden found out through one of her spies—a helper who buys toiletries for her—and, at lunchtime in front of the entire dorm, called her a whore and grounded her. She made the girl an outcast, chastising anyone who tried to be nice to her.

Jay speaks to Devi for the first time. "It's okay," he says. "Maybe another time."

Nair Sir walks Devi to the dorm, which is close to where the buses park. It is dark and the mosquitoes are insatiable. Devi swats one on her arm and a swollen mound rises under her skin.

Nair Sir says, "You should apply Odomos so you don't get bitten."

"I'll ask my grandfather to buy me some next time I'm at his house."

"I'll get some for you tomorrow."

"Thank you, sir."

It is something her dad would have told her, to put on mosquito repellent. One day when Devi was five, she was running around the house wearing socks that were too big for her, and she tripped and fell against a door. The hinge made a deep gash on her upper lip. Her dad rushed her to the hospital and insisted the doctor stitch up the cut so she wouldn't end up with a scar. After arriving at boarding school, Devi was convinced that her days of being cared for that way were over.

Devi looks forward to Maths Club every week. Homework doesn't feel like something she does in isolation anymore. She thinks about Nair Sir. And the club. They are all on the page with her. Nair Sir telling her about the beauty in transforming equations, Govind calling her a genius, Tina carelessly putting her arm around her, Jay sitting by the window, glancing at Devi frequently. Nair Sir meets students at their level. He has incredible patience with Jacob's apathy. He takes Devi beyond ninth-grade maths. He sneaks in quadratic equations while listening to Tina talk about her dad, who works in America and has visited only once in two years.

Months pass like this, then Tina invites Devi to her sixteenth birthday party. Devi isn't supposed to go to her grandparents' house on weekends, but she convinces them to let her come so she can go to the party. Tina is a feisty, unsettling thing. Aware of her many admirers, she is quick to tease them but isn't interested in any of them. She knows what she wants so clearly; she has sorted out her life's plan: go live with her dad in the US for college, marry an American, and settle down in one of those *Full House*–style white homes with a flight of stairs that leads to a red door. Tina can come across as self-serving, selfish even, because she talks about herself a lot. But if she likes you, she will make you feel special in ways few people can. She takes on the role of an older sister, teaching Devi how to use hair remover cream, shape her nails, and pluck her eyebrows. She lets Devi tag along with her during lunch breaks. Imagine that: an eleventh-grade student, especially someone like Tina, hanging out with a ninth-grader!

The party is at a café Devi has only seen from outside. She has seen groups of students laughing uninhibitedly on the patio, so comfortable with one another. A large sign displays the name of the café in cursive bubble letters: AMBROSIA.

Devi wears a brick-red skirt and a cream floral top with shoulder pads. She's borrowed her aunt's battered leather purse for the occasion. She takes the bus to Archies Cards and buys a birthday card and a small teddy bear for Tina. She gets the bear gift-wrapped and takes another bus to the café. She underestimated the time it would take to get there and is late by half an hour. She goes up the stairs leading to the café, holding the wrapped gift. The air is thick with a yeasty golden smell.

Tina spots Devi from the patio and stands up, waving.

A large group is sitting around three conjoined tables. Devi recognizes Nair Sir, Jay, Govind, and Jacob. Tina has many other friends Devi has never seen before. She is delirious with all the attention.

"Look who's fashionably late," Govind says and smiles at Devi.

Jay has saved Devi a spot. She is the youngest person there. She feels like she is still being tested to see if she's worthy of being in their circle.

"Are your shoulders always like this," Govind says, "or just for special occasions?"

"Stop pulling her leg," Tina says and steals some of Govind's fries.

Nair Sir is seated across from Tina at the centre of the table. He asks Devi what she wants to eat, and for that she is grateful. He is having coffee and veggie puffs, so Devi orders the same thing. "Please order whatever you want," Nair Sir says, laughing. "Our Tina here is very rich." Tina rolls her eyes. How different it is to see Nair Sir outside of school. He's wearing the same kind of clothes, but his shirt is untucked. Does he have a wife? Kids? How lucky they would be to have him as their dad.

As they get ready to leave after a few hours, Nair Sir tells Devi, "You're looking nice today." He's standing beside her on the landing. The rest of the group is on the stairs, saying their goodbyes. Jay lingers for a bit, and then leaves. It is almost dusk. The neon lights turn on, and the name of the café is illuminated in red and white. A breeze ruffles Nair Sir's hair, which makes Devi smile.

Tina drove her car, but she offers to wait with Devi for the bus. Nair Sir is taking the same bus as she is. Standing between them, Devi thinks how lucky she is to have met these two people. The wall behind the bus stop is plastered with movie posters.

"Have you seen *Titanic*?" Devi asks Tina.

"Not yet," Tina says. "I don't like to watch movies when there's so much hype. But I'd watch it just for Leo." She pauses and looks at the poster. "Look how symmetrical his face is." She lets out a heightened sigh.

"I really want to watch it," Devi says. "I love the Céline Dion song so much."

"My heart will go on and on and on …" Tina sings out of tune and laughs. "If you want, we can all go to the movie. Even Nair Sir will come. He has nothing else to do on the weekends."

"You rat!" Nair Sir says.

When the bus comes, Nair Sir gets on through the men's entrance at the back. Devi gets on at the front door and finds a seat. She turns around and sees Nair standing at the back, holding onto a strap. He smiles and gives her a soft, slow nod. Devi looks out the window and feels him watching over her.

• • •

During maths club, Tina suddenly announces, smirking with her look of effortless superiority, "It's actually called *math*, not maths. That's what they say in America."

Nair Sir responds quickly, "Oh right, the American beauty queen says it's math, so from now on, everybody call it math only." The way he says it, stressing the "th" like he's spitting, makes them all giggle. Even Tina.

Summer vacation will start soon—the week after final exams—so when Nair Sir steps out, Devi brings up *Titanic*. She doesn't want to come across as desperate, but she wants to see it before she goes back to Saudi Arabia and her parents.

"Watched it twice already. Mainly for Kate," Jacob says with a covert grin. "But I don't want to see dumb people freeze to death again."

"Me neither," Govind says.

Ash and Ash say they watched it together a few weeks ago. Jay says he's leaving for Dubai, where his parents work, the night of their last exam. Tina doesn't say anything, but after the others leave, she tells Devi, "I know I said I'd go with you. How about the Sunday after finals?"

Devi nods vigorously. "Should we ask Nair Sir?"

"I think he went to feed the stray dog," Tina says and chuckles. "I'll make sure he comes."

As Devi walks to the dorm, she sees Nair Sir at the edge of the courtyard, the dog by his feet. He calls out to Devi and tells her to wait. "I know these will be your first final exams here in this school. Do you feel confident?"

Devi smiles and nods.

"You're a superstar! You don't need my help," he says, "but one thing I will tell you. Please reserve fifteen minutes at the end to check your answers. That is the single most important thing. Not just in maths but in every subject."

"Yes, sir. Thank you."

"So, what are you doing for your summer vacation?"

"I'm visiting my parents in Saudi Arabia."

"You'll be gone for two months! I'm going to miss you. You have to give me a photo so I can remember you when you're gone."

After final exams, Devi's grandparents come to school to pick her up. Before he leaves, Jay hands her a note with his address—in case she feels like writing to him, he says. Devi drops it into her bag; she has no intention of keeping in touch with him over the summer. Her flight to Saudi Arabia is on Tuesday. Devi is too excited to pack, thinking about going to the movie with Tina and Nair Sir.

On Sunday morning, she calls Tina to ask her where they should meet.

"I have a chest infection," Tina says. "I can't come."

Something hot travels up Devi's face, into her eyes, her ears. She holds the receiver in front of her face, staring at it in disbelief.

"You could ask the group, but I don't think anyone else wanted to go."

When Devi doesn't answer, Tina says, "Sorry, love. I could go with you next weekend."

"I'm leaving for Saudi Arabia in two days," Devi says curtly.

"Well, you could still go with Nair Sir," Tina says. "But I don't know."

Devi phones Nair Sir at his home. She has called him only twice before to ask maths questions. She expects someone else to pick up the phone, but again, it is him. He asks, "Do you want to go?" He lingers at *go*, like he wants her to say yes.

Devi says, "Can you ask Ash and Ash to come?"

"I'll call them," he says. "But are you sure you want to go? I mean, if they don't come."

Devi pauses, and then says yes.

Devi takes the bus to the theatre. She's wearing a short black top and a flowy black and white skirt—Tina gave her the outfit because it didn't fit her anymore. It is the most stylish thing Devi has ever worn.

Nair Sir is waiting alone outside the theatre. Something about him is different, not in his appearance but in the way he makes her feel. Her breaths come out in short bursts—fear and excitement, and an anger she cannot understand, coming together in her lungs. Nair Sir tells her he couldn't reach anyone.

He takes his wallet from his shirt pocket and buys the cheap tickets. Devi's dad would never buy those tickets. Nair Sir doesn't get her popcorn. This makes her angry—her father always gets popcorn! She notices that people are staring at them. A group of men smiling weirdly. An older woman's eyes brimming with contempt. A few young women turning around to look at them more than once.

Devi realizes Nair Sir is too young to look like her dad.

They squeeze by rows of legs to get to their seats. Devi sees more people staring at them. She suddenly thinks about the warden finding out about this. When she sits down beside Nair Sir, she immediately regrets it. The seats are so close to the screen, Devi is practically looking up at the ceiling.

Nair Sir is quiet throughout the film. So is she. She wants to enjoy the experience, but she can't stop thinking that she is alone in the dark with Nair Sir. He is on her right, and Devi leans to the left as far as she can, her hand nowhere near the arm rest. It is nothing like watching a movie with her dad.

On the massive screen, Rose asks Jack to draw her like one of his French girls. She strips down to nothing except a necklace with a blue pendant. Jack tells her to sit on the couch. Her breasts look large even when she lies down. He instructs her to put one arm behind her on the couch, and a hand by her face. He begins to sketch her.

Devi moves her body forward and even farther away from Nair Sir so that he doesn't come into the vicinity of her vision. She cannot believe that a child would be allowed to watch this, even under parental guidance. She has never watched such a film, never seen a woman in the nude. Her ears are burning. She cannot believe that Tina didn't warn her of *this* scene. What is Nair Sir thinking? He has not said a word. Unsavoury noises arise from corners of the theatre. She feels like she is about to throw up. She has never wanted so badly for something to end.

When they leave the movie theatre, Nair Sir walks in front of Devi. He seems small. She doesn't look at him while they wait at the bus stop. The black shirt she is wearing is made of a synthetic fabric and she can feel the sweat soaking her back. A woman next to her in a cotton saree is counting exact change for the bus ride. A vendor calls out in singsong, "Kaapi, kaapi, kaapi." Devi doesn't turn back to look at Nair Sir when she gets onto the bus. She doesn't say goodbye.

Devi sits in the front seat, beside the driver. The bus

rumbles and starts. Two thin trails of smoke emerge from the sandalwood incense sticks perched on the ledge underneath the windshield and disappear into the air, merging with the smell of sweat and exhaust fumes. Devi turns her gaze outside, looking at the people on the sidewalk appearing and disappearing. The bus picks up speed, and the city churns. Buildings give way to trees. Rice fields clip by like a fast-motion picture. The sky darkens, and so does the inside of the bus.

Driving Lessons

HERE IN OUR OFFICE lunchroom, I have made friends. Now, there are two kinds of Indians who move to the US: one who transforms drastically in their appearance, in their manner of speaking, in their preferences, and the other who fiercely remains the same.

Pinky was in the former category. After living in the US for over ten years, she dressed like an American, spoke with an almost American accent, and was concerned with things like Jamba Juice running out of wheat grass. She was light skinned for an Indian and bleached her hair. She had expensive nails—the clear, glossy ones with white tips. She said with pride that people often mistook her for a white person. While a part of me judged her for concealing her Indianness, for being enamoured with everything American, another part of me wondered how it would feel to trans-form like that. Turn into a new person.

Bhanu, however, spoke with a distinct Telugu accent, never pronouncing things in a way that would make it easier for an American to understand, wore her hair in a braid, and did not try to hide the thick gold and black mangalsutra around her neck, the marker of a married Hindu woman.

I didn't want to be either of them. Besides, I was only here temporarily for a work project, unlike the two of them—Pinky, who had made America her home, and Bhanu, who seemed like she was on that path. But did I want to go back to Hyderabad and share a two-bedroom apartment with five girls?

"I'm not married, and let me tell you, I'm not that young. I'll be thirty-two this December," was how Pinky introduced herself to me. "My father and Mummy don't talk to me anymore. They're back in Chandigarh, and you know how folks in India are. If you don't get married by thirty, you're old. I'm too headstrong to just get married to any rando they find for me. I like my independence. But when you're past thirty, you do begin to feel that instinct to settle down. Bhanu, you would know, right?" Pinky said, winking at her. "What about you, Devi? How old are you? Twenty-five?"

"I'm twenty-two," I said, not knowing how I was being judged.

Bhanu's family had also disowned her because she

married a Muslim, I later found out, but she never talked about it. Bhanu seemed more content than Pinky, like she knew who she was and didn't need to prove it to anyone. She was also more reserved. She walked around with a little notebook, scribbling in it every now and then. When I found out she was working on a novel, I liked her immediately.

"There's a story in me," she said. "I need to get it out."

The three of us had nothing in common, but these two women, each a decade older than me, became my first friends in this country, the ones who got to watch me as I learned to become who I was supposed to be.

This is how I taught myself to drive: I would take my red Ford Focus, rented by the company I worked for, and with printed directions from MapQuest drive slowly to someplace new every day of the week. Take a right at Bryan Avenue, and then make a left or a right at Jamboree Road. Jamboree cuts the city in half. If you drive all the way south, you can get to Balboa Island, either by ferry or by the bridge across Beacon Bay. Irvine is the kind of master-planned city that, at the time, I had seen only in aerial shots in Hollywood movies. The city leaves nothing to chance. Adobe-style apartment buildings are fashioned into neat C-shaped units, squares, or arches. With hardly any high-rises, the sky is open and wide and a stunning blue.

At first, I would only go as far as the Target on Jamboree or the Starbucks by the mall. As I grew bolder, I started driving on El Camino to Interstate 5. And in this way, suburban California revealed itself to me, one block at a time.

Learning to drive gave me something to focus on, brief moments of control as I shed parts of myself that I had come to resent. It was as if I were back in boarding school, looking for a place where I could belong. My heart palpitated a little every time I turned onto a new road. I hadn't yet taken a driving test in California and barely knew the rules of driving in the US. So I had Bhanu show me the basics—how to drive on the right side of the road, stop at a STOP sign, use the indicator instead of honking as we did back in India, leave a car-length between me and the vehicle in front of me, recognize one-way streets, and merge onto freeways.

This left me with scores of incidental things to find out on my own. Like how at a left-turn light, sensors detect whether a car is waiting, so unless you stop close enough to the intersection for the sensors to work, the left-turn arrow will never turn green. Once, I waited at a left-turn light for more than fifteen minutes. A long line of cars began to honk behind me. I put my car in park and stepped out to ask the driver behind me what the problem was. Shaking his head, he gestured for me to move closer to the intersection.

Another time, as I merged onto I-5, my heart pounding like a boom box, I missed a woman on a motorbike in my blind spot, and I was too slow for the guy in a convertible behind me. The woman on the motorbike swerved left, passed me, and turned around to call me a fucking asshole. The man behind me, fortunately, hit his brakes inches from my car, changed lanes, and slowed down to flip me the bird—with both hands! As disoriented as I was, I was in awe of his ability to momentarily let go of the steering wheel completely on the highway. I steadied my car and my heart, stayed in the right lane, and held my breath for a mile.

Later that week, Bhanu bought me a small statue of Lord Ganesha from Little India in Artesia and stuck it to my dashboard. For protection.

Our office had a dress code: women wore pantsuits or skirt suits (never without pantyhose). But Bhanu and I were in IT, which was out in the annex (we were riff-raff, our manager liked to say), so we could get away with button-down shirts and khaki pants. If we had to make a presentation outside of the annex, we carried a blazer. I bought mine at Macy's for sixty dollars. That's as much as I had paid monthly in shared rent for my apartment in Hyderabad.

Pinky was a business analyst, so she was on the fourth floor of the main building, wearing tailored pantsuits. This one time, when Pinky returned after a weeklong vacation, she sent a message on the office chat: *Girls! Meet me at my cubicle. Urgent!*

I had finished most of my work for the day and Bhanu, who was having a slow day, was scribbling in her notebook. We grabbed our blazers, replaced our sandals with dress shoes, and sprinted to the elevator.

"I bet she found someone and is getting married," Bhanu said as we got off at the fourth floor.

Pinky was seated, her breasts spilling out on her desk. She spotted us, stood up, and said, "What do you think?"

Though she appeared different—instead of a pantsuit, she was wearing a pencil skirt, beige pantyhose, and under her blazer, a tube top instead of a shirt—I wasn't sure what I was supposed to be looking for.

Bhanu said, "Oooh là là. Sexy! But why did you call us here so urgently?"

"Come on, guys. Can't you tell?" Pinky said. "I got a boob job!"

She took my hands, placed them on her chest, and said, "Feel them."

Bhanu found it hilarious, me feeling Pinky's new breasts out of obligation. I politely retrieved my hands and made fists with them.

"You know, I've always been self-conscious of them," Pinky said. "But then I thought, I have disposable income, no mortgage, no kids, so this is a problem *I* can throw money at."

Then she whispered, "All the white girls have big boobs, have you noticed? They get boob jobs as birthday presents from their moms before they turn twenty." She shimmied, and her breasts shook like Jell-O. "They're a bit numb, though. The doctor said they'll start developing some sensation soon."

Staring at Pinky's cleavage, Bhanu said, "But is this allowed? As per our dress code?"

"Well, as per our dress code, you can't wear khakis, but there's no mention of tube tops." Pinky scrunched her face at Bhanu. "Here, you feel them."

"No thanks." Bhanu interlaced her fingers behind her back and held them there until we left the fourth floor.

Back at the annex, Bhanu took out her notebook. "My goodness, that woman. I have to write this down," she said. "You can't make this stuff up."

Not long before I travelled to America, I got myself an international driving permit, which allowed me to rent a car in almost any country. I had moved to Hyderabad a year before, right after college. I had driven my dad's old stick-shift Hyundai Santro in Trivandrum a handful of times for the sole purpose of taking the driving test. The test involved traversing the lines of an H with the car: drive up the first vertical line to the tip of the H; back up halfway down and turn ninety degrees, the car in reverse; travel the length of the horizontal line; then turn ninety degrees again, still in reverse, to cover the bottom half of the second vertical line; then drive forward to the tip of that line. It required a lot of practice, but it was the *only* test needed to get a driving licence. That and a three-thousand-rupee deposit to the man outside the gate of the Road Transport Office got me the glossy international driving permit, or the IDP, as he fondly called it. I never found out if the money was a bribe or the fee.

I say I travelled to America, not moved, because at the time I thought it was temporary, a short work trip. I was at that age when you don't think beyond a few months at a time. I didn't say goodbye to anyone. I took a taxi to the airport, with all my belongings in two suitcases, a few hours before sunrise, the sky dark as tar and a new heat in my throat. I had just broken up with Jay, who looked like Tom Cruise from *Top Gun*. He was a motorcycle enthusiast, a gamer, and someone who had a hard time graduating from college. Jay is six-foot-four, and I am five-foot-(almost)-one. When I met him in Maths Club at boarding school, I was fourteen and he was sixteen, and I thought I had time to grow a few inches. We were in the club for different reasons—he was struggling, and I was looking for a challenge. Our romance took off after he graduated from high school, both of us infatuated with our ideas of each other. We rarely met in person because we were no longer at the same school, but we wrote to each other or talked on the phone regularly. In the seven years we were together, I didn't catch up to him vertically. I didn't realize then how small I felt standing beside him.

When we communicated through handwritten letters, our relationship was alive, our love enormous, but after I got a job in Hyderabad and moved miles away from my parents' home in Trivandrum, we both got used to text messages and emails, and the only thing that held us together—this idea of romance—began to wither away. The things we had written about in letters, which we handed to each other discreetly, seemed silly as text messages or, worse yet, in long-distance phone calls we had to pay for ourselves. My career was taking off, while he was having a hard time finding a job. We began to fight like a bitter married couple. During one fight, he called me a whore. I knew instantly that our relationship was over, but it took me more than a week to come to terms with what I was about to do. I broke up with him by email the following week. I slipped away to California a few weeks later.

Pinky often talked about her relationships in great detail, and I found myself filled with desire. That raw want to be touched. To be kissed passionately. To feel the weight of a warm body on mine. I found myself thinking about sex a lot. In meetings, in the shower, in the grocery store. I was working long hours and only meeting men at work. Most of them were married, and of the two who weren't, one was twice my age. The other guy, Roy, was tall and good-looking but married to his work. The two of us were once tasked with finding a new intern for the web development team. Between interviews, Roy told me things he liked in prospective candidates and things he absolutely hated.

"One of my biggest pet peeves is when they use the word 'stuff,'" he said. "'So, what did you do in your previous job?' 'Oh, I did HTML and JavaScript and stuff.' What kind of a professional uses the word 'stuff'?"

Roy said this with so much passion that I was compelled to agree with him. But after that conversation, I was left worried I'd end up using the word in front of him. That Friday, he asked me what plans I had for the weekend, and I said, "Nothing much, laundry, cooking, cleaning, and *stuff*." I couldn't avoid the word. Heat pooling under my face, I excused myself and ran to the washroom.

With driving, I was having better luck. I started to experience the high that came from successfully taking the freeway to the mall at the other end of the city without missing an exit. As a rule, I would not leave the house without either printed or handwritten directions. I had a

Nokia phone that only made calls or sent text messages. In the beginning, because I wasn't familiar with the concept of the freeway, once I missed an exit, I never knew how to get back on. I would call Bhanu, who would guide me, step by step, back onto the freeway. As time passed, I got more comfortable and experimented with trying to memorize directions.

I might have gotten overconfident because the next Sunday, I decided to drive to a Trader Joe's at the other end of the city without directions. On my way, I saw a hair salon that advertised in pink neon letters: WAXING AND THREAD-ING AVAILABLE and remembered that I hadn't gotten my eyebrows done since I'd arrived in the US. The receptionist asked me if I had an appointment, then after looking at the empty store said she could take me. She guided me to the back room and threaded my eyebrows herself. Inches from my face, she smelled of woody perfume mixed with the garlicky smell of falafel.

After that, I stopped at a Hallmark store to buy a card for Bhanu for her upcoming birthday. Bhanu's parents never called her, not for birthdays or the New Year or Diwali. My parents called me once a week, and my father emailed me every day. Sometimes they were blank emails with a simple *Good Morning* in the subject line or a movie recommendation. Sometimes they contained weird trivia about cars or videos of funny animals.

When I finally left Trader Joe's, it was dark. As I got on the freeway, I was thinking about an imaginary boyfriend. I kept driving, imagining how effortlessly witty I'd be. He'd open the door of his car for me. He'd hold my hand as we walked into a nice restaurant. Somewhere between entering the restaurant and leaving, I missed my exit. I began to see unfamiliar signs, and the idea that I was lost because I had been dreaming about something frivolous like a boyfriend made me feel like an idiot.

I took the next exit, turned right, and kept driving until I got to a strip mall. I called Bhanu, but it went straight to voice mail. I called Pinky, but she didn't pick up. I drove around in the dark, trying to find the way back to the highway, but I only got more lost in identical-looking streets. Then I called a cab. The cab driver parked and waited for me to get in. I explained that I simply needed him to drive to my apartment, and I would follow him in my car. But the driver, an older Indian man, told me that was ridiculous. I don't know why my proposal annoyed him so much—I was still going to pay him—but it seemed he thought it was beneath him to make a passenger-less trip. Or perhaps he was mad at the ineptitude of a fellow South Asian. In any case, he eventually agreed. When I paid him outside my apartment, he muttered something under his breath and did not respond when I said thank you.

That night, the power went out at around 11 p.m. I hadn't

planned for this because one of the promises that America made was that there wouldn't be power outages like there were in India. I didn't have a candle or a torch. (The following day, when I asked the man at the convenience store if I could buy a torch, after a lot of back and forth, he corrected me, telling me I needed a flashlight.) And then my phone died. At this point a sadness enveloped me and I found myself crying for the first time since I had broken up with Jay.

I was living alone for the first time in my life, and I hadn't thought about it until now. I felt a nostalgia for the frequent power cuts in India, in boarding school, at home in Trivandrum, and in our apartment in Hyderabad, surrounded by my friends or cousins or roommates, huddled around a candle amid a swarm of mosquitoes. We condemned the power cuts and the government that was responsible for them, but then we would sing old Hindi songs or play Antakshari, or listen to our grandmother tell the same stories over and over again. Sometimes the aunty next door came over, wearing her loose cotton nightie, bringing her four-year-old son, and she would tell us about her drunk husband's latest antics. Sometimes we watched street dogs making love in the moonlight.

When the power returned, the spell was broken and we would get back to whatever we were doing—studying, cooking, watching TV. There was always so much noise that you couldn't feel alone. Now, alone in my apartment, all I could hear was the sound of my own sniffles—isolated puffs of wind. Cries for help.

I never had anyone over to my apartment except Bhanu and Pinky. I was thinking about inviting the new family that had moved in above me: a man, a woman, and a little girl. My balcony was right below theirs, so sometimes I'd see bubbles the little girl was blowing floating down. Sometimes I'd see them out on the street, the little girl in a wagon pulled by her mother. I heard their cooking noises, TV, vacuum cleaner. And their arguments. Sometimes, in the quiet of the night, I'd even hear passionate sex noises (I marvelled at how freely the woman screamed).

I don't know how things might have turned out if I had invited them over that weekend.

I was separating my whites for the laundry when I heard the first scream. At this point, I thought the couple was having sex again, but it was just after noon. I heard the woman scream again. I opened the door to my balcony. The little girl sat on a chair on their balcony, reading a book as if her life depended on it.

The screams got louder. I heard another voice, an older woman's voice. "Don't do it! Don't do it!"

"Get out of my way, you fuckin' bitch!" I heard the man say.

I was struggling to understand what was going on.

"Fucking whore! You think I don't know what you're up to?"

The woman's screams sounded like an injured animal's. I heard a lot of running and pushing upstairs. I had never called 911, but I knew from movies that I had to. When I went to grab my phone, I heard a loud pop.

Afterward, there was silence.

Then I heard the older woman screaming, "He killed her! He killed my girl."

There was stomping outside my door, so I looked silently through the peephole. The fish-eye view of the hallway and the staircase was blurry and dark. I saw the man from upstairs run down the stairs, and then go back up again. Then I heard a series of objects falling, followed by sharp thumps. Other doors in the hallway began to open. I heard dragging and screaming. I couldn't make out everything the man was saying, but I thought I heard him wail, "Why'd you make me do it?"

Two days later, on Monday, I stepped out of my apartment for the first time since the shooting. No one had bothered to clean the trail of blood on the staircase.

Everything I had come to take for granted since I moved to this country: driving after dark, living alone, coming and going as I pleased—every ounce of entitlement, of invincibility—was up for re-examination. I didn't speak about the incident to anyone at all. There was too much intimacy in such an act of violence to discuss it with anyone at work, even Bhanu and Pinky. And I didn't want my parents learning about it and worrying about my safety. My confidence in driving took a beating, and I began to ask myself what right did I have to drive in this country, to be safe, to feel safe?

My international driving permit was set to expire, so I booked an appointment with the DMV for a driver's test. On the day of the road test, it was raining—auspicious, my mom would have said. My examiner was a lean, serious-looking man with a swift gait. As I waited in my car, the rain beating down on the windshield, I watched him get into three different cars. All three drivers returned from their test looking disappointed. When the examiner got into my car, it suddenly occurred to me that I hadn't driven with a passenger in this car before. I got flustered and asked him if the temperature was okay. The examiner ignored my question, said his name was Bob, and asked me to drive out of the strip mall. Then he told me to turn right, his voice listless. He kept silent throughout, except to ask me to change lanes a few times, making notes on a paper attached to a clipboard. By the time he asked me to merge onto the freeway, I had lost all my confidence, and the car began to slow down instead of speeding up. There weren't any cars in the right lane, so I merged slowly.

The only words Bob uttered on the freeway were, "The speed limit is sixty-five miles per hour, not thirty-five." It didn't seem that he was stating a fact, but rather as if he was laying out my fundamental flaws.

When we returned to the strip mall, he said, "I'm sorry, but as you can tell, you didn't pass."

I told him I had just gotten nervous, that I was a good driver.

"You were going at least thirty miles below the speed limit, you didn't check the road when you drove through a green light, and you slowed down before changing lanes every time. What driving school did you go to?"

"I didn't go to driving school."

"Who taught you how to drive?"

"My dad taught me in India, and then I practised by myself."

"That explains it. Get a driving instructor."

I don't know what came over me, but I started the car and pulled out of the parking spot. Bob told me to stop the car, but I told him nicely that I just wanted to show him what I could do. He stared at me like I had lost my mind. I drove carefully to the end of the parking lot where there were no cars, and I did the full routine. There was familiarity in each turn, and I was very calm, but Bob's face turned pink as he begged me to stop the car. When I was finished, I said, "I just made an H with the car. Would someone who doesn't know how to drive be able to do that?"

At the DMV, I was told that I would not be allowed to use my international licence unless I had an experienced, licensed driver beside me. That night in bed I cried, thinking of all the things I had lost in the past year.

The next morning, I found a driving instructor on the internet and explained my situation. I didn't tell him about the H.

Imran was a Pakistani man perhaps as old as my dad. He told me to take his car out for a spin. I turned into Culver Drive, drove for a few blocks, made a left at Irvine Boulevard, drove all the way to Jamboree, then turned into Bryan and back to Culver.

"You're a good driver," Imran said.

I wanted to hug him, but he continued, "The problem is that these examiners are looking for specific things. Like you drove by a railway crossing. The gates were open, but what if a train was coming? You could have killed us both."

I must have looked horrified because he said, "Don't worry. You have great control over the vehicle. We just need to fix these optics. We'll practise twice a week for two weeks, and you'll be good to take the test again."

When I went back to the DMV for my second road test, Bob was standing at the end of my line. He said, "I'm going to have you switch to the other line with Brenda."

• • •

My driver's licence arrived in the mail five business days later. In the picture, I looked like an excited teenager, my eyes wide open, my short bangs curling in. I took a photo of it and emailed it to my dad. He replied right away: *good job.*

Three weeks later, I was driving on the Pacific Coast Highway, going no place in particular. I felt safe in the car, hidden behind steel and glass. The road snaked alongside the mountains. I thought about the little girl from the apartment above me and wondered if she was safe now. The Ganesha statue Bhanu had given me caught the light of the sun.

I drove over a bridge that made me feel homesick for a place I'd never been to. It was crowded with people who had stopped to take pictures. Then I followed a road leading into a little coastal town, driving onto a strip with gift shops on both sides. At the end of the road, the Pacific Ocean emerged, an immodest blue.

I parked my car and stepped out. As I stood there, the whole world became perfectly all right, water lapping, gulls calling, and in this beauty, in this moment of clarity, the sun began to go down, setting the surface of the water on fire.

Surya, Listen!

THE DIFFICULTY WITH MAKING PLANS, Bhanu thought, is that the looking forward to something is always better than the thing itself. She said it out loud to herself, and then wrote it down in her notebook. The notebook where she often found half-baked ideas and mediocre sentences, and occasionally a line she was proud of the next day. This was a habit from a long time ago, when she had wanted to become a writer.

Bhanu had spent the last few months planning this trip with her husband and son—her teenaged son's first trip to India—and now she wondered why she had thought it was a good idea. Her son, Surya, liked routine and the comfort of daily, repetitive tasks.

She opened the blackout curtain in Surya's bedroom and found a note beside his backpack. She read it and tossed it into the trash can. Bhanu watched as Surya squirmed, squinted, and upon seeing her, broke into a big smile. The child, a stocky boy of fifteen with coarse stubble, stretched, exposing a thin, cakey line of dried drool on the dark pillowcase.

"Good morning, Surya," he said, welcoming himself to this new day.

Everything about the morning went as planned, until Surya decided he wanted to wear his house slippers to the airport. Bhanu's husband, Imran, explained to Surya all the ways in which house slippers were impractical for air travel.

Surya repeated to himself, "Surya, listen! Surya, listen!" which was something he did when adults tried to reason with him, but he had no intention of listening.

Bhanu knew that once Surya decided to wear house slippers, he would wear house slippers or they would miss their flight, so she told Surya he could wear them. Surya smiled at Bhanu, then stuck his tongue out at Imran and did a little dance.

Imran brought two fingers to his eyes in a V, then pointed them at Surya in the *I'm watching you* sign. Surya giggled and dashed out of the room.

"If he starts losing his shit on the plane, I don't know you people," Imran said. "Surya who? Bhanu who?"

Bhanu laughed, wondering what it would be like to not know Surya, to not be a mother, his mother. "The new headphones should help. That's what the doctor said."

"Did you pack the cotton balls? And the iPad?"

"Yes," Bhanu said, putting a pair of Surya's sneakers into their carry-on. "Coffee's on the counter."

"I'll take out the garbage first," Imran said and went to empty the bins in all the rooms.

From Surya's room, Imran called, "Bha, he's getting very cheeky. I found a note from his teacher in the trash."

Bhanu went to Surya's room and found Imran holding out the piece of paper she had tossed. "That wasn't him," Bhanu said, and she switched to a squeaky voice as she recited what was written in the note. *Surya was disruptive during recess again. Again, he kicked Liam on his shin.*

"*You* threw it away?"

"I'm sick of her, Immy. Surya would not have kicked Liam if Liam didn't keep tapping him on the shoulder. He hates that kind of stimulation. I've told the teacher a million times. Why doesn't she stop that?"

"Well—"

"She's more concerned about the optics of how kids like Surya are perceived and less about how they move through life," Bhanu said. "She raised such a hue and cry at the school board about the use of the term 'special needs,' championing the use of the word 'disabled,' as if it sounds any better. If she tried to understand how Surya's mind works instead, it would make a big difference."

"At least she's trying to help. What's wrong with the word 'disabled'?"

"Why are you taking her side?" Bhanu said, her voice soaring and her words quickening. Over the years, she had seen the terms used to describe children like her son evolve from "mentally retarded" to "intellectually disabled" to "differently abled" to "special needs" to "disabled." "What's wrong with it is that it assumes that there is a standard, a normal, that Surya doesn't meet. Why can't these children simply be referred to by their names, or just as *children*?"

"Okay, okay, Bha, you're right," Imran said, wrapping her in a hug.

They got to board the plane early because of Surya. He walked behind Imran and in front of Bhanu. From the back, he looked like an older person, with his large, droopy shoulders and his limp. He had started growing a beard at fourteen, possibly because of all the medications he was taking. Imran shaved it for him whenever Surya let him, but today was not one of those days.

Bhanu would have preferred the window seat, but they were in the middle four-seater. Surya sat in between them, his knees touching the tray table in front of him. He started bouncing his feet and shaking the seat in front, saying, "Surya, listen!" before Bhanu or Imran could stop him.

When the passenger next to Bhanu arrived, she was hunched over, digging for the noise-cancelling headphones in her large handbag, which was tucked away under the seat in front of her. She looked up to find a boy with a backpack and a binder settling in beside her. Despite the navy blazer he wore over his T-shirt, he didn't look a day over twelve. He put his passport and boarding pass inside his backpack.

"Are you travelling by yourself?" Bhanu asked.

"Yeah," he said. "My family's coming tomorrow. I'm going to London for a competition." His speech was businesslike, his sentences crisp.

"What kind of competition?"

"It's a math competition called the Olympiad."

"The International Mathematical Olympiad?"

"Uh-huh. I'm one of six participants from the States."

"Well, we just have a stopover in London," Bhanu said, chuckling, processing what the boy had said. She was rarely in the presence of someone like him, someone who would probably move through life with ease. "We're going to India to visit my parents. I haven't seen them in fifteen years."

The in-flight announcements drowned out the passengers' voices. Tray tables needed to be secured, seat belts needed to be fastened, phones needed to be switched off.

"Forgive me for asking, but how old are you?" Bhanu inquired.

"I'm fifteen," he said, trying to make his voice deeper.

"You're the same age as my son," Bhanu said, looking at Surya, who was observing her as she spoke to the boy.

She wondered what it took to raise a child who had been selected from millions to participate in an international competition.

Imran cleared his throat. Bhanu turned back to the boy and said, "This is my husband, Imran, and my son, Surya."

The boy leaned forward to catch a glimpse of Surya and Imran. Surya said, "Who's the best? Surya is the best!"

Imran turned toward the boy, "It's nice to meet you—"

"Dev," the boy said, fingering the hem of his blazer. "Hello."

When the plane began to taxi, Surya started rocking back and forth nervously. Bhanu secured two cotton balls in his ears to ease the discomfort of the pressure difference as the plane ascended. She knew from experience that cotton balls were harder to throw across the aisles than earplugs. Surya held his parents' hands and started to scream. Now that his voice was breaking, his screaming sounded like a pack of coyotes howling.

Bhanu offered earplugs to the passengers close to them, saying, "He'll settle down once the plane is in the air."

After Surya fell asleep, Dev said, "You're a good mother."

Bhanu understood the implication—she was a good mother because she had patience with this crazy man-child. Usually this kind of comment annoyed her, but it felt strange coming from a fifteen-year-old who knew nothing about motherhood. What did they say about motherhood? It is like having your heart outside your body for the rest of your life? Actually, it was more like your heart takes the form of something unreliable, something floaty—like a helium balloon with a mind of its own. Bhanu wrote this down in her notebook.

For as long as she could remember, Bhanu had dreamed of writing novels, sweeping family sagas that would become cult hits. But she was also a realist, so her plan was to have a steady job, save money, and then write in her free time. When Surya was a baby, in the darkness of Bhanu's maternity leave, she swore to herself that she wouldn't turn into one of those mothers who have no life beyond their children. Who lose their sense of purpose after the last child leaves home. The way her own mother lost her purpose when Bhanu first got married and moved out.

Bhanu's mother never forgave her for divorcing her first husband and marrying someone like Imran. Bhanu tried to reconcile with her mother when Surya was five. Her mother, who declared that she had sacrificed her life for Bhanu and asked what Bhanu had given her in return. "You go and marry a Muslim, even though I beg you not to, and then see what happens?—you get a sick child," Bhanu's mother, who refused to use words like "disabled," but was fine with "not right" or "abnormal," explained.

Bhanu thought about countering her mother, throwing facts in her face, but she stopped herself. Her mother's cruelty that day affected Bhanu the way it always did—it gave her confidence in her choices and a sense of calm, because she knew that she had done the right thing leaving when she did. Leaving her first marriage, leaving her parents' home, marrying Imran, leaving for the US, all against her mother's wishes.

Imran was unremarkable in all the good ways. Everything about him was average—his short and boxy stature, his common Indian face, his mild personality—except his capacity for quiet kindness. She likes to tell him that she married him for comfort and fell in love with him after.

He disagrees. "You married me for my body," he says, doing some biceps curls, showing off flabby arms, which always makes her laugh from her stomach.

After they bid goodbye to Dev at the London airport, Imran said, "What fifteen-year-old speaks like that?"

"He gave me his *business* card." Bhanu fished it out of her purse and showed it to Imran.

DEV DESAI

MATHEMATICS AFICIONADO

DEV@DESAISFORYOU.COM | 555-788-9001

"My brain hurts," Imran said, cupping his head in his palms.

Bhanu fingered the business card and said, "This reminds me of Sai and her balloon-artist phase."

"Please don't talk about her," Imran said, the light leaving his face.

"Come on, Immy. It was so long ago."

"I don't want to be reminded."

There was never a reason for Bhanu to imagine someone like Sai. Bhanu met her at the Indian grocery store. Sai was walking down the vegetable aisle, so focused on finding what she was looking for that she didn't realize her cart was blocking Bhanu. When she turned around after bagging her bunch of curry leaves, she was startled to see Bhanu standing there, and she froze up like a child caught stealing candy. Sai had smooth, youthful skin and golden-brown eyes with thick eyelashes. Her frame was petite and her body was droopy. Her nails were bitten to the quick. It turned out that Sai and her husband lived in the same apartment building as Bhanu and Imran. At the time, Bhanu was thirty-two (Sai must have been twenty-two). She had moved to the Bay Area to work in the IT department of a casino after her previous work contract in Irvine ended.

In the apartment building, there were five to seven Indian families at any given period who were in Bhanu and Imran's primary social circle. There were some who had been in the US for years and others who had recently arrived. Bhanu and Imran were in between, having already applied for their

green cards. Most of them worked in IT, administering data-
bases and building websites and implementing enterprise
applications. Week after week, they cycled through the same
conversations—visa status, career advancement, babies, and
the situation of their friends in India who hadn't made it the
way they had. They were all looking for the same things:
something in common and scraps of hope.

Sai didn't obsess about planning for babies or fulfilling the latest prerequisites for a green card application
or upgrading from an apartment to a house. She was
somewhat socially awkward. She couldn't read social
cues—when people wanted to change the topic, or if they
were hinting they wanted an invitation to her house for
the next get-together. Or that it was okay to discuss certain
topics in front of some people but not others, depend-
ing on their personal situation. People talked behind her
back in an unkind way, but Bhanu didn't indulge in these
conversations. She saw Sai as a little sister who needed
protection.

Sai went through odd phases. That summer, she got into
making soaps and her apartment was covered in lye and oils.
Another time, she was developing a serum for Indian hair.
And then there was the balloon business—that one lasted
the longest. Her husband built her a website and bought her
a DSLR camera to take pictures of the balloon arrangements
she made in the small guest bedroom of their apartment.

The smell of latex never left that room. Sai went to every balloon conference in San Francisco, spent hours on online balloon forums, and made herself business cards with the title: BALLOON ARTIST. Balloon garlands and decorations for baby showers and corporate party packages were her most popular offerings. Most people in their circle—the ones who would never have had the courage to put themselves out there like that—made fun of Sai behind her back, until she started bringing in real money.

One weekend during the height of Barack Obama's first presidential campaign, when most of California was on a high, Sai made $2,500. She threw a celebration in the building's party room. There was a shift in power in their social circle. What Bhanu remembers the most from that time is the distinct smell of latex. And morning sickness. When Bhanu entered her second trimester, Sai got pregnant. The balloon business slowed down. The two women, ten years apart, were expecting their first babies.

Bhanu took twelve weeks of maternity leave, and when it was time for her to go back to work, Imran's mother came over from India to care for her grandson. Soon after her arrival, the apartment started to smell like the inside of the armoire in Bhanu's childhood home. Although Bhanu tried to convince her mother-in-law that there were no cockroaches or lizards here, she still went about stuffing mothballs into her folded sarees and petticoats.

Bhanu spent her days writing her novel, which was growing limbs and contorting, becoming a large, complicated creature. A character resembling Sai started taking shape—a little eccentric, perplexing, and unpredictable. Bhanu had the habit of reading her work out loud to Imran, especially if she was proud of it. In those days, he used to say, "You are obsessed with that woman!"

"I am not," Bhanu responded. "You have to admit, Immy, she's interesting. I've never met anyone like her. If she puts her mind to something, she is so relentlessly focused on it."

"I don't know what it is, but she's always seemed a little off to me. Like there's something wrong in her wiring," Imran said. "And besides, why don't you write about your handsome husband?"

Bhanu rolled her eyes and said, "Because he talks like that!"

After Imran's mother went back to India, Sai offered to babysit Surya when Bhanu was at work. "I am home taking care of Prabhu anyway, so why would you send Surya to a daycare and have strangers look after him when he's so little?"

Bhanu offered to pay her, but Sai refused. After a lot of insistence, Bhanu convinced Sai to accept half of what the daycare would have charged. Imran did not like the arrangement, but Bhanu assured him it would only be for a few months, no more than six, until she found a really good daycare for their son.

Six months became a year, and then two. Bhanu had every intention of moving Surya to a daycare, but the idea of sending her baby to be with strangers seemed painful now. Besides, Surya was thriving with Sai. He had started talking at nine months and could count to twenty by the time he was one. Sai was very keen on teaching the boys math, and Surya picked it up faster than Prabhu.

Bhanu's wants had been so outsized then—the perfect family, money, success, fame, her son enrolled in the best schools in the country—the best of everything.

A week after Surya turned three, Bhanu came to pick him up after work. When Sai opened the door, her face was as pale as a blank sheet of paper.

It was little Prabhu who said, "Surya taking long nap."

At first, Bhanu thought Sai was acting cold because she hadn't called her all day. She tried to lighten the mood, saying, "Finally, he tired himself out enough to nap!"

Sai said they had gone to the park and when they came back, Surya had told her he wanted to sleep. Her words sounded stilted, like she had rehearsed them.

"Prabhu didn't do nothing. Surya taking long nap," Prabhu said.

Bhanu ran inside without taking her shoes off to find Surya lying on the bed in the guest room, motionless, surrounded by pillows. Bhanu shook him, but he wouldn't open his eyes. She picked him up, but his thirty-pound body hung from her hands flaccidly.

Bhanu called the paramedics. Surya had a faint pulse, and she held on to his wrist as if that would keep him alive. Bhanu clutched his small frame, heavy and unmoving, her chest splitting. From the bed, where she sat with her son, waiting, Bhanu could see inside the closet that held the helium tank. Red and green balloons tied with ribbons touched the ceiling. The room was steeped in the smell of latex.

With great effort, Bhanu allowed Sai into her field of vision. She was standing at the threshold, so unsightly and pale. Bhanu said that she wouldn't report her if she explained what had happened.

Sai had been inflating balloons. Afterward, she got the boys dressed for the park and gave them each a balloon. Out in the hall, while her back was turned as she locked the apartment door, she heard Prabhu ask Surya for the red balloon. Surya didn't give it to him. Refused outright. Prabhu pushed him. Surya fell down the entire flight of stairs. Sai took Surya back inside, gave him a nighttime Tylenol, and put him to bed. Ten minutes was all it took.

In the back of the ambulance, Bhanu wrapped her arms around herself, biting into the flesh of her hand. Pain to muffle the agony inside her. Bleeding with regret. In that moment, Bhanu thought of the red balloon that had escaped, unharmed, grazing the ceiling of the landing, the ribbon swaying slightly.

For weeks, Bhanu and Imran sat by Surya's bedside at the hospital, watching his quiet body for any sign of movement. It was still, like a starless night sky. There was no telling he was alive, other than the rhythmic crests on the heart monitor, which Bhanu began to see in her dreams. Every now and then, the doctor came to check on Surya, peeling back one eyelid, then the other. These thoughts ran through Bhanu's head: How Surya was perfectly fine when she dropped him off at Sai's that morning. How anyone with a head on their shoulders could have made such a devastating chain of decisions. How falling down a flight of stairs could cause so much damage.

There was no way to prepare for something like this. Bhanu's arms had to be wrapped in gauze, and she had to be sedated in order to sleep. The inside of her right hand would be scarred permanently with crescent-shaped bite marks.

Bhanu and Imran didn't talk much. The only way for them to survive was to focus single-mindedly on Surya's recovery. Bhanu researched different rehabilitation paths. She prayed for hours at his bedside, read to him, massaged his small arms and legs. She made a deal with God—she would throw out her novel, along with all her other outsized wants, in return for her son's life. It now seemed ridiculous that she had ever wanted so much.

Surya came out of his coma after three searing months. His neurologist said that he would be bedridden for the rest of his life. Bhanu took a year's leave of absence from work. For Surya's rehabilitation, she used every dollar available from her insurance company, took advantage of every free program offered by the city, and paid for anything that wasn't covered. Imran let Bhanu take the lead in Surya's care. For the first time in their marriage, he was okay with not sharing the load. He was livid that Bhanu refused to take legal action against Sai.

"Will that give us our old Surya back?" Bhanu asked him.

"That's not the point. How can you be okay with that woman walking free?"

Every year after that, around Surya's birthday, Bhanu obsessed about why Sai had done what she did, and about how Bhanu had missed any signs that Sai could do something like that. Bhanu wanted to be able to explain it to herself so she could forgive Sai.

A few years later, Bhanu tracked Sai down on social media. Sai was using an old picture for her profile, perhaps from the time when Bhanu first met her. She was wearing a turtleneck and leaning against an old Nissan, her arms crossed. Bhanu stared at Sai's picture. She saw all the things she had seen before—the perfect nose, the strands of curly baby hair sticking out of her tight bun, and those big golden eyes.

She remembered something her mother-in-law had said when she met Sai briefly during her stay: never trust someone with cat eyes. Bhanu had written this down in her notebook. Sometimes she would take out all the notebooks she had gathered over the years and read them. She used to say there were stories in her, but now she wondered if the story was in her or if she was in the story.

Surya became Bhanu's full-time job. When she went back to work, she negotiated with her boss to work from home as much as possible. She gave up her hopes of being promoted and did the bare minimum to keep the job for the health benefits it provided Surya. Bhanu and Imran were isolated from their friends' circle. Bhanu's new friends were the steady stream of physiotherapists, speech therapists, doctors, and nurses who cared for Surya. In a year, he was able to sit and hold himself up. In three years, he started to walk, although he had a limp. Slowly, he relearned how to speak.

In time, Imran came around. He began to see Surya's recovery through Bhanu's eyes. That it was possible for them to work toward something without knowing if they would ever get results. The brain damage had caused changes to Surya's face: his eyelids drooped, and bags developed under his eyes. By the time he began relearning how to walk, he was six years old. He was much heavier, his centre of gravity was higher, and his falls were more painful to watch. But it gave Bhanu much more joy than when she first saw him walk as a toddler.

Surya was able to perform basic personal tasks by the time he was ten or so, and Bhanu was consumed by a deep sense of melancholy. She didn't know what to do with herself. She couldn't concentrate on work or household tasks. She lay awake beside Imran, night after night. She started seeing a therapist. She had spent all those years blocking Sai from her thoughts. And now she knew she would need to feel that ugly thing called forgiveness to be rid of her.

At London's Heathrow airport, the screech of suitcase wheels and the wails of babies and the repetition of announcements merged into an indistinguishable, reverberating hum. The three travellers waited, tiredness and anticipation setting in, causing Bhanu and Imran to become snappier and Surya cheekier. The child started kicking the carry-on suitcases until they toppled over, all the while saying, "Surya, listen!" to himself. Imran scolded him, and Bhanu stood the suitcases up again and tried distracting him with games on the iPad, but he only grew more irritable.

Finally, when Bhanu said she would get him a cupcake, he settled down, and they grabbed their bags and walked in the direction of the stores.

They found a café where live music was playing. The singer, a beautiful young woman in a short blue dress and big hoop earrings, sang into the microphone, strumming a guitar. Imran bought a chocolate chip muffin for Surya, coffee and croissants for Bhanu and himself. The music had R&B and jazz influences that put them in a mellow mood as they had their breakfast.

"I ran into her a few years ago," Imran said.

Bhanu looked up from her coffee. "Sai?"

Imran nodded. "At a Trader Joe's. She was shopping with her son. What was his name?"

"Prabhu," Bhanu said. "Why didn't you tell me?"

"I didn't want to remind you."

"It's not like I would forget," Bhanu said, wiping chocolate from Surya's face. The child, mesmerized by the woman's singing, stared at her and smiled. "Did you talk to her?"

"She saw me and her face turned red. She looked like she was out of breath, almost like she couldn't stand straight," Imran said. "I think she was having a panic attack. I got her some water."

"Why didn't you tell me this, Immy?" Bhanu said.

"I told you why. Sai looked miserable and scared. I asked

her why she would do something so stupid. I couldn't help myself."

Bhanu stared at him, and then at her coffee, absorbing every word he was saying, finding meaning in each syllable.

"She started to cry, standing there in the beverage aisle," Imran continued. "She said that she had panicked, that she was so afraid to get in trouble. She said she looked up to you, that you were the only one who thought anything of her, and she didn't know how to tell you she had made a mistake." Imran's round face creased up, the bags under his eyes looking more prominent under the bright café lights. "She thought the problem would go away if she ignored it."

"She didn't make a mistake until she ignored it," Bhanu said.

Imran cleared the table except for their coffees, which were still full. The song ended and people clapped and cheered. The young woman started a soulful number, her eyes fixed on the ceiling. Surya smiled, his eyes gleaming, as if he could experience all the pain, all the beauty in his life, and still be happy.

In the boarding area at the Mumbai airport, Bhanu and Imran waited for the last leg of their journey to Hyderabad. Surya had fallen asleep on one of the chairs, his long legs splayed out. A couple squeezed past and sat across from them. They looked about the same age as Bhanu and Imran. The man wore a black blazer, although it was hot; the woman wore a satin blouse and black pants.

The couple told them that they ran a college prep institute in San Jose, California. "We help students prepare for the SATs, build winning applications, and write standout essays," the man said. He sounded as if he'd given this pitch thousands of times.

"These days, there are so many institutes, but we started in 1998, so we have a lot of experience," the woman added.

"How old is your son?" the man asked.

Bhanu said he was fifteen. Imran indulged the man, asking him how many kids came to the institute every year and how their results compared before they arrived and after they left.

When the business-class boarding was announced, the couple stood up. "You absolutely need help in today's climate. The competition is too high," the man said. "Here's my business card. Call me when it's time. Better sooner than later. I'll give you a discount."

The card read EXEL UNI PREP and on the back the man had written 10% in blue ink.

"For sure," Imran said and shook the man's hand. "We'll call you when it's time."

After the couple left, Imran stuck out his tongue and pretended to retch at the conversation they'd just had.

Bhanu laughed so hard, thinking about the man and his ridiculous institute.

Bhanu watched Surya as he slept, the slightest of smiles creeping up the edge of his mouth. She wondered what he was dreaming about.

Suddenly, Imran said, "Sai didn't know that Surya had survived."

"What?"

"Yeah. She thought we lost him. She kept crying, saying she was sorry. She said that she hadn't had a good night's sleep since that day because she believed she had killed a child. She was depressed for years and her husband grew tired of her and left them."

Bhanu imagined Sai weeping, her golden eyes filled with tears. "You told her that Surya is okay, right?"

Imran was quiet. Then he sighed.

"You didn't tell her?"

"At least she should have that punishment," Imran said. "Living with that guilt."

Bhanu woke Surya as the economy boarding was announced. She looked up at the giant papier mâché pigeons hanging from the ceiling.

"I feel sorry for Sai," Bhanu said.

"So you forgive her?" Imran asked.

Bhanu shrugged.

Forgiveness wouldn't come to her fully realized one fine

day, Bhanu thought. It would come slowly, drop by drop, through choices she would have to make. She looked at Surya and felt all the love inside her brimming to the top in a way that made little else matter. No one could take that away from her. Bhanu was astonished by the beauty, by the fullness, by the joy in the little life her family had built for themselves.

Morningside

IT HAS BEEN TEN HOURS since Tito's last cigarette and we're walking a tightrope—he's driving, I'm praying, and our three-year-old son, Akash, is asleep in the car seat the morning of New Year's Eve.

I wish Tito would take a break to smoke, but he's doing this thing now where he pretends he's not a smoker. Going on these mysterious walks every few hours and always smelling of baby wipes smothered in nicotine. I don't know who he thinks he's fooling; I have the nose of a bloodhound.

We merge onto the 401, a stretch of highway that cuts through downtown. We have a six-hour drive to Montreal. Could be nine if there's traffic, so we are leaving pre-dawn.

"Are you mad at me?" I say, and regret it immediately. What conversation that starts like that has ever gone well?

He scoffs. His expression is the same as it always is these days—furrowed eyebrows, sunken cheeks, downturned mouth.

"No, like really? Are you still upset about the paper towels? I'm sorry."

"As if." Another scoff.

I have known him long enough to know that "as if" means "as if you care." I look out the window and sigh.

The city is choking in snow and salt. Highway 401 does its best, and despite what it's been through—ceaseless traffic, decades-long construction, snowplows, and multi-vehicle collisions—it's still standing. The Toronto skyline appears— the needle of the CN Tower sticking out like an exorbitant dream—and then disappears, and stretches of emptiness begin.

I try to remember what I liked about Tito. We met in grad school in Orange County, years before we moved to Toronto, him with a few years of work experience and me right out of undergrad. He ignored me for a whole semester. The more he ignored me, the more I was curious about him. His intelligence was seductive. The way he talked about mergers and acquisitions or cash-flow analysis—full of passion—turned me on. And that something like that turned me on made me feel smug about myself. He hardly registered my existence, or if he did, he didn't let on.

Soon after first semester, I was diagnosed with a lung

infection that wouldn't go away. Constantly going in and out of doctors' offices and hospitals, I began to lose my friends. They didn't know what to do with me. My father, who had lived in Houston all those years I was growing up in Trivandrum, had recently moved back to Kerala. I reached out to Tito once for help with the coursework I had missed. From then on, he attached himself to me like industrial-strength Velcro. He moved his class schedule around and drove me to every doctor's appointment. He was interested in me in ways no one had ever been before— he wanted to know how my day was, who I spent time with, what I was reading, what I ate for dinner, where I had lived before, who I had dated, who my friends were. I'd had so many admirers back in school and in college, but this felt different; it was all-consuming.

Tito didn't share a lot about himself, but when he did, it felt like an invitation to an exclusive club. He told me that he was named after the Yugoslav revolutionary by a great-uncle who was a lifelong communist. As a proud capitalist, Tito resented his name, but I loved it. Tina and Tito had a good ring to it. I used to call us T-squared. Whenever I said something silly, he would say, "Oh, Tina, Tina, Tina," and I would love the sound of my own name.

On Sundays, Tito would pick me up and we'd go on these long drives on the Pacific Coast Highway from Santa Monica to Balboa. He had a used silver Chevy Malibu back then. We would roll down the windows, open the sunroof, and pretend we were in a convertible, singing badly. "I swear the sky is wider and bluer and freer in California," I'd say, and he would look at me with lustful eyes. We would stop at a Starbucks, then take the ferry to Balboa Island. He would drive the car onto the ferry and kiss me the entire sailing until we got to land. At the beach, he would smoke a cigarette or two, and I would take selfies of us on my flip phone.

I lost those pictures, all of them. If only I'd been more careful.

As we pass Scarborough, I see an exit named Morningside Avenue. Orange clouds border the edge of the sky. I push back my seat and try to relax.

"I once read this book called *The Glass Palace*," I say. "There was a rubber plantation in it called Morningside, somewhere in Burma or Malaya. I don't remember the story that well, but isn't Morningside such a lovely name? It sounds so nostalgic yet hopeful, like you'll always have something to look forward to there. When we buy a home, we should call it Morningside."

Tito stares ahead, eyes glazed.

"What do you think?" I rub the back of his neck.

He shakes my hand away and says, "About what?"

"The name Morningside. Do you like that name?"

"What difference does it make?"

"If you tried, it would make a difference."

"As if I'm not trying. Why else would I agree to this road trip?" He stresses "road trip" like it's a curse word.

"This trip alone won't fix things. You haven't been doing anything Linda asked us to do, yet when we're at her office, you act like everything is okay."

Linda's office is on the second floor of a heritage house rezoned for commercial use. There are no windows, just three chairs, a couple of vapid paintings, a small coffee table with a box of tissues. The first time I entered, I thought it looked like a collection room in a sperm bank. I kept expecting Linda to suddenly produce magazines with boobs and butts. Tito is always on his best behaviour at her office. Whenever I bring up fights, he says, "You're right," or "I'm sorry, I'll do better," and Linda thinks he should get the Best Husband Award. In the end, it always seems like she's suggesting that I need individual therapy and there's nothing wrong with him.

"You think Linda is going to fix this?" he says and eyes the space between us.

In an effort to see how we can turn this trip around, I go back over last night's events. Tito went on a walk, which is code for a smoke, at 7 p.m. and came back in a decent mood. At dinner, I asked him if he could put his phone away. There was no fight; he just ignored me and kept scrolling.

Akash did a demonstration of how to eat spaghetti properly, slurping every noodle, his mouth, nose, and chin splattered with marinara sauce. Then I put Akash to bed—an hour-long process—and Tito was asleep by the time I was ready to join him.

This morning, he woke up angry. When I said, "We have to stop to buy some paper towels for the drive, just in case," he asked, "What's wrong with you? Why do you always leave things to the last minute?"

"You could have thought of it, too."

"I was babysitting all afternoon while you were working late yesterday!"

"It's not babysitting when it's your own child," I said.

When it's bright enough, we stop at a rest area for breakfast. I wake Akash and get him into his winter coat while he's still in the car seat. He smiles and says, "Are we there yet?" I say no and tickle his stomach. Inside the building, I contemplate the lines in front of Tim Hortons and Starbucks before choosing Tim Hortons—the line is longer, but they have six employees whereas Starbucks has only three. Tito has disappeared, and I am relieved. A cigarette will do more for this marriage right now than anything else.

The entire place smells like burnt coffee—metallic and acrid. We wait in line, the serpentine disarray of groggy travellers stupid (or smart) enough to travel on New Year's Eve snaking to the end of the building.

Akash holds out a hand, spreads his fingers, and says, "High-five!" I give him five.

"Up high." I give him another five.

"Down low." He pulls his hand away. "Too slow!"

Over and over. Each time, it's a giggle fest.

I get coffee, chocolate milk, oatmeal, and bagels. I know Tito's standard order—he is not a fan of change—sesame bagel, toasted with butter, and a latte. Akash proudly helps me carry the food to a table.

"Where's Daddy?" he asks, suddenly noticing that Tito hasn't been with us.

"He probably went to the washroom," I say.

As we sit down, I see Tito emerge from the side of the building and wave at him. He goes and sits on one of the couches. *Oh yes, I forgot, these chairs are too hard for his soft ass.* In the hospital the night Akash was born, when I was in pain after the episiotomy, Tito complained constantly that the guest bed in the maternity room was too hard.

Akash and I grab all the food and move to sit beside Tito. I fold a corner of a napkin and tuck it into Akash's sweater. He gets started on his bagel and cream cheese. I hate eating on a couch because you have to balance the food on your lap, but I am trying. Linda says a bit of compromise can go a long way. There's nothing wrong with this relationship:

no affair, no meddling in-laws, no physical abuse. So we have to make it work.

"Please, let's get along, okay?" I say to Tito softly as I open the lid of my oatmeal.

"Look who's talking."

"Why are you acting like this?"

"Well, it depends on the people around you."

"Stop referring to me as *people*. If something is bothering you, tell me, and we can talk about it. If not, can we just try to enjoy the trip?" My head is pounding.

"I'm tired of this shit."

"Shhh! Akash is here. What are you tired of? I don't understand."

"You never understand anything. That's your problem."

"Goodness, what's *your* problem?" My oatmeal tastes like wet newspaper.

"You don't care about me one bit. All you care about is your work, your friends, your yoga classes, your book clubs."

"Don't yell. Just because I care about other things doesn't mean I don't also care about you. Give me an example of a time when I made you feel like I didn't care about you."

"Leave it. No point."

"No, tell me."

"Mommy, look!" Akash says. "A reindeer." He points at a pitiful animated reindeer on TV, advertising sugar cookies.

"Awww, isn't it so cute, kanna?" I turn toward Tito again. "I always ask you to come do things with me. And I'm the one who's always planning things for us to do together. What are you so upset about?"

"Leave it!"

"You always do this. You get me all worked up, and then you end the conversation as you please." I hear my voice getting progressively more nasal. "When you get home from work, you go straight to the couch and have a four-hour date with your phone. You don't even look up from that thing when I talk." I hate who I turn into when I'm with him.

Tito sighs his long, drawn-out sigh.

Akash sings, "Rudolph, the Red-Nosed Reindeer."

I don't remember exactly when things between us started to deteriorate, but it was probably around the time when my health started to improve. Tito was a good sick person's boyfriend. He needed to take care of someone, and as I got well, he started to feel like he wasn't needed anymore. He measured his worth based on how much I needed him, not how much I wanted him. Sometimes, when things between us got much worse, I had to lie in bed and pretend to be sick to get some kindness from him.

In the beginning, I misread his erratic mood swings—the

yelling followed by kindness—mistaking them for passion. He has a manic energy about him. And when I started to achieve success at work, his insecurities grew. I never knew which Tito I was going to get on any given day. We fought with as much passion as we made love, most often in that order.

The litmus test for love, I had read in a book, is this: *You know you love someone when you love even their dirty socks. If you don't, you should get out.* According to that definition, I should have left years ago. I can't stand the dirty socks, the bad breath, the coffee rings by the bedside. Sometimes I think I have no business being married.

As we pass Kingston, Tito says, "Sorry if you were hurt."

It's an annoying apology. How about: *I'm sorry for hurting you?* But I take what I can get. It's probably the nicotine kicking in.

"Remember that gelato place in Kingston?" he says. "Best gelato we ever had."

Not true, but I agree. The best gelato we ever had was, of course, in Rome. Also, the best pizza. The best mozzarella. The best sex. This was pre-Akash, on our honeymoon. We spent only two out of the ten days fighting; the rest were magical. I remember how he rested his hand on my shoulder as we waited in line. I remember how I looked, especially in that green dress and that ridiculously big, overpriced straw hat. I must look for that dress. I hope I didn't get rid of it.

I would never admit it to Tito, but my love for him dwindled rapidly after Akash was born. In contrast to Tito and all his tantrums, Akash was a calm, low-maintenance baby. How do people have more than one child? My friend Nicole has six kids. I don't know how she does it. Not the taking care part—well, that, too—but how does she share the love? Nicole left her first husband, with whom she had three kids, each a year apart, when she found out he was cheating. And a year later, she met this new guy with two little kids of his own, and they got married and had one more child. She tells me that she went from one miserable marriage to another.

Akash is wide awake and bored. He says he needs to use the bathroom. We stop at the next rest area and I take him to the ladies' bathroom because he still sits to pee. I help him take off his mittens and his coat, making sure he doesn't touch or lick anything he shouldn't, and hold on to his gear as we wait for a free stall. As soon as he sees the toilet, he is suspicious. "Does it flush by itself?"

It is clearly an automatic toilet, but I try to ease him into the stall. "Maybe. But remember what Mommy told you? If you don't move while you're sitting, you're good."

"No! Remember at the airport? You said the same thing, but it flushed by itself when I was peeing."

I spend the next fifteen minutes convincing Akash that I will pick him up immediately if it starts flushing mid-performance. Eventually, he relents and sits on the toilet.

I wait in position, ready to scoop him up at the slightest swoosh.

After a few seconds, he says, "Never mind, it's not coming. Let's go."

In Montreal it's an obscene minus twenty-eight degrees Celsius. Tito lets us out in front of the hotel entrance and goes to find parking. He wants to take us for lunch to a pasta place he used to frequent when he worked here for a year before we were married. When we get there, it is closed. So are most of the other restaurants and cafés.

"This is the problem with Canadians," he says and shakes his head. "Where Americans see opportunity, Canadians see work-life balance."

In the end, we eat overpriced, over-al-dente pasta at the hotel restaurant. "This mac and cheese is so hard," Akash says and scrunches up his face.

It is too cold outside to do anything, so we decide to check out the hotel pool. It is nothing like how it looked on the website.

"I can't believe we drove for ten hours to do this," Tito says.

Akash splashes water at him, and Tito splashes back like he doesn't mean it.

I bounce Akash on the water and ask him, "Do you want to sit on Daddy's shoulders?"

Tito balances Akash on his shoulders, but he is so tall, Akash is barely in the water. Akash says he wants to come down and swim by himself. He's wearing orange floatie armbands as big as his head. Splashing and giggling, he says, "This is the best day of my life." The irony lands heavily on my chest.

Akash says, "See, Mommy, if you fart, bubbles come up." His eyes pop at the discovery, and he and I laugh for a long time.

Tito's face is inscrutable, and Akash's joke fails to induce the slightest smile. He wipes his face with a towel, his eyes red from the chlorine, and sighs.

For New Year's Eve dinner, I've made a reservation at a fancy vegan restaurant. I help Akash take off his snow pants, jacket, mittens, earmuffs, and scarf. The place is stunning, with massive chandeliers, floral Victorian-style wallpaper, lots of plants, even a vintage typewriter.

As I admire the decor, Tito says, "This would have cost, I would say ..."—he does some quick mental math—"about $250,000 to set up. But think about it: the place is packed, they probably make an average of $2,000 a night, at least. That would be about $56,000 a month. Imagine that!"

He does this every time we go to a nice restaurant. Now I'm putting a dollar value on everything instead of enjoying the experience. I see dollar amounts hanging above the waiters and the bottles in the bar. Once, I asked Tito if he dreamed of opening a restaurant and he said, "Crazy or what? That's too risky."

It's not that I haven't thought of leaving him. Some days, I fantasize about it—walking away, never having to see Tito's face again. But I keep thinking that he will snap out of it, that we could go back to knowing only enough about each other to be able to like each other. Also, I've done the math: the financial, emotional, and physical toll of a separation and a custody battle with someone like him would offset any potential future happiness.

After dinner, the three of us walk around, waiting for midnight. There will be a New Year's celebration at the pier in Old Montreal. When we were newly married and Tito worked in Montreal, I used to visit him on the weekends and we'd bike along the cobbled roads.

We stop by the Notre-Dame Basilica and take pictures in front of its Christmas tree. I've taken this picture so many times I don't care anymore. Akash is tired, I am freezing, Tito is fidgety. He picks up Akash, who falls asleep on his shoulder. We decide to skip the New Year's celebrations and go back to the hotel.

I am relieved. After we put Akash to bed, I suggest we watch a movie on Netflix. I get out my laptop and set it up in the corner of the room, so as to not wake Akash.

"What do you want to watch?" I ask.

"What's the point?"

"Can't you put in some effort here?" I say. "I am so tired of trying so hard all the time. Every single trip is like this. I am so sick and tired of this."

"Fuck you!" he yells. A glob of spit lands on my forehead and drips down my eyelid. I look at Akash. He is still fast asleep.

I wipe my face on my sleeve, take my phone, and leave the room. I go down to the lobby and sit on a couch in the corner. Large bamboo palms sit in massive pots by the entrance. I watch couples walking by on the street, holding hands, imagining what they might be saying to each other, painfully aware that I am no longer one of them.

There's a countdown in the lobby. At the stroke of midnight, lovers kiss and teenagers scream, jumping up and down, as fireworks erupt outside. At the centre of my chest, a cavity.

The concierge discreetly brings over a box of tissues and whispers in a French accent, "Hang in there. It gets better."

The man is a stranger, but in that moment, I feel that he understands me better than anyone else in the world, especially Tito—the man I married and have given hours and weeks and years of my life to. I cry harder because I frantically want the words of the concierge to be true.

After an hour or so, I go back upstairs.

When I get to the room, Tito says, "I was about to wake Akash and come looking for you. Called you many times. Are you okay?"

I check my phone and it is dead.

Tito leaves the room, presumably for a smoke. I lie down silently beside Akash. The cavity inside me grows bigger and bigger until I am entirely hollowed out.

The next day, we go to the indoor botanical garden. The walk from the parking lot to the building is dreadful. The road is icy and the wind makes me want to scream. But inside, we discover various themed greenhouses, each with its own microclimate. We move from a temperate to a tropical to an arid climate as if travelling through different lifetimes. We are hit by an astounding humidity in the Tropical Rainforest greenhouse, with its crotons and hibiscus and bromeliads, amazed by the colour and symmetry of the flowers in the Orchids and Aroids greenhouse. As we move on, we encounter cacti and succulents in the arid atmosphere of the Hacienda greenhouse, complete with a pool and adobe-style terraces.

"This reminds me of Santa Monica," Tito says. "The stucco walls and the rounded doorways. Remember the street where you used to live?"

"Feels like a lifetime ago," I say.

"We always had good weather then, right?" he says.

Nothing about leaving is easy.

With each agonizing lawyer after another, Tito becomes increasingly irate. He does everything in his power to stop me—showing up at my friends' homes, sobbing and saying how much of a shock it was for him, how I didn't give the slightest indication that something was wrong. It makes no sense to anyone in my life that I am doing something so drastic. Tito uses Akash for leverage, and it brings me to my worn-out knees. I am in a constant state of palpitation, and the sound of Tito's footsteps unravels a mania inside me.

And then one day I lose my balance, fall down the stairs, hit the bottom. A shooting pain spreads from my tailbone throughout my body. I am all alone in the house.

I lie unconscious until Tito comes to drop off Akash. I am taken to Emergency and a battery of tests are done, faster than I have ever experienced. My lung disease has returned, and this time it is cancerous.

For the rest of our time together, Tito oscillates between caring and ruthless, confusing me to the bone. I will leave a few years after I get better, but on the day Tito takes me to my first chemo treatment, he buys me snacks for the hour-long drive to the hospital. He's got a blanket for me in his car. From the hospital room, I can see him leaning against the car, chain-smoking, looking inconsolable. I take a deep breath and think about my lungs, and how I never smoked a cigarette my entire life.

The Many Homes of Kanmani

THE FIRST THREE BODIES I saw at the hospital weren't my mother. When I finally found her, bile snaked its way up my throat, choking me. It looked like they had put my mother's clothes and her worn gold chain on a monster. Eyes swollen shut, lips like balloons, face a bluish grey. I want to remember her face the way I saw it that morning on our way to swimming lessons, her smile that revealed the gap between her front teeth and her eyes that told whole stories. But always, that bloated creature comes to mind.

That was six years ago, when I was eight. My mother had signed me up at the swim school at the other end of the city, forty minutes away, because the pool was nicer. My mother never learned how to swim, so this was a big deal for her. While the other parents were on their phones, my mother would watch me through the big glass window. If I glanced her way, I would see her looking at me, clapping.

In the bathroom that morning, she did my hair. Using a thin comb, she drew a line from my nose up my forehead and over my head—chasing symmetry—parting my thick hair in half all the way to the back of my neck. She brushed each side until you could run your fingers through it without getting stuck. She braided both sections and twisted them into two tight buns using Love-in-Tokyos, which were these elastics she got from India, each bun bound by two glossy blue beads. She moved her head from side to side, squinting, to make sure the buns were equidistant from each other. These things were important to her.

In the car, we played the word game. You have to say a word starting with the last letter of the previous word. Whoever says the most words wins. We started playing this game so that my mother could improve her vocabulary—in English, that is. Sometimes, we gave ourselves constraints— we could only use nouns or names of animals, things like that. That day, it was toilet words. I started us off with fart, then toot, then turd, then dump, then poop, then pee, and so on. I was on a roll, and I had to pause just to get all the giggles out.

There is a spot on the highway where the road dips. My mother and I used to pretend it was a roller coaster and scream with glee when we drove over it.

English escaped my mother, always running away, running in circles. She had a degree in Tamil literature, and speaking Tamil is like making honey. In the ten years my mother was in the US, no one would give her a job because they couldn't understand what she was saying. But my mother was full of meaning, and the people she came across became full of knowing for having met her. She could get to the point quickly because she knew only a few words. But that wasn't the kind of language people who were hiring were looking for.

My father was a truck driver, which was like having a father only on paper. He was gone for days, sometimes weeks at a time. My mother insisted that I go to a Montessori school—you know, the kind where each child is supposed to learn at their own pace. Looking back, I realize this was probably why my father had to work so hard. The school was in another neighbourhood a half-hour drive away. I was the only daughter of a truck driver amid the kids of lawyers, dentists, realtors, and engineers. I know this because the teachers assigned us a project in which we had to write what our parents did for a living.

Mrs. Erin told me to write "Stay-at-Home Mom" as my mother's profession and "Trucker" as my father's.

Corey, who was also eight, but still reading at a grade-one level, read my father's profession as "Fucker," which the kids found hilarious.

When I told my mother about this at pickup, she had to look up the word on her phone. She said, "Good. We have a new word for 'F' for the word game," and we laughed louder than necessary. She kissed me on both cheeks, right there in the parking lot. Unlike other moms, her love was always out in the open for everyone to see.

Her love was also full of Tamil. She used to call me kanmani. Precious, the apple of her eye. I have forgotten most of the Tamil I used to know, but sometimes in a crowded place I'll hear some family talking in Tamil, and the words will come back to me, along with my mother, unharmed.

The rain came out of nowhere. It was like nothing I had ever seen before. The wind was howling, and my mother struggled to keep the car steady. She clung to the steering wheel and became very quiet. Water pounded the windshield like stones, and the wipers went wild.

The road had turned into a river, and we were afloat in it. The water hid the dip in the highway. Suddenly, we were underwater. Thick, grey-black water that climbed inside our old Honda Civic, soaking my dangling feet. My mother let go of the steering wheel, ferocity in her eyes. She opened the door and we abandoned the sinking Civic.

She yelled through the howling wind and pelting rain, "Kanmani, you see that railing there? There *is* a railing there.

Imagine that's the end of the swimming pool. I want you to swim over there and hold on to that railing. Understand?" That was the last time I was a child.

I held on to the railing for hours, days, I don't know. By the time they reached me, I was so hungry I asked for food before I asked for my mother.

Millions of people took to the streets after that hurricane. All the homes that had been swallowed up by the storm were in poor neighbourhoods. Enough people had died to create an uprising. A new president had just been elected, and he travelled to all the ruined cities and gave the *thoughts-and-prayers-we-will-rebuild* speech. The same one he would give four more times that year, and so many times in the years to come that I stopped counting.

I was taken to the hospital and then to a group home while they tried to find my father. It was days before someone removed the Love-in-Tokyos from my head, and by then my hair had hardened into the shape of the buns. Twin lumps of coal refusing to be flattened.

Who brings an eight-year-old to identify a body? I think the system had collapsed by then and nothing mattered anymore. Weeks after I found my mother, they told me they had found my father's body in some creek down south. I told them I didn't want to see another monster.

Around that time, I was moved from the group home to a foster home with this woman named Carly, who was into climate change protests. She was in her thirties and lived alone in a house that looked like it was going to collapse from the outside, but the inside was decorated all colourful and cozy. Purple futons, colour-block curtains, hanging ferns, walls filled with paintings and posters. Looking back, I see that she really wanted to make me happy without expecting me to do anything for her, like give her a sense of fulfillment.

I told Carly about this South Indian restaurant my mother had taken me to once where they served idli and sambar. She found it on the internet, but when we got there, we learned that it had closed permanently, like many of the businesses in that part of town after the hurricane. This made me so sad I began to cry like a baby—the first time I cried in front of Carly. She must have thought I was so shallow for crying about something like food, but that is what you cry about when you have no one left.

Carly was one of those people who simply cannot stop talking about the *thing*. The thing that is their life's purpose. For Carly, it was the environment, and she talked about it all the time, to people who would listen and people who wouldn't. Our neighbour used to say Carly could never keep a boyfriend because she was always going on and on about emissions, fossil fuels, this and that. Once, when our neighbour was babysitting, she told me that Carly had met this man named Tito fifteen years ago at a clinic where she used to work. They had a whirlwind romance—he bought her flowers and gifts and spent all his time with her. They were engaged within a month and an intense and tumultuous relationship followed. But Tito looked down on Carly's environmental activism and always took the side of big corporations, making light of all the concerns she raised. Their relationship reached a tipping point when Carly had a stillborn baby. Tito blamed Carly, saying she hadn't been careful enough, she was just a hippie who could never be a good mother. After he left, Carly devoted herself entirely to her activism.

Unlike my teachers, both at the old Montessori and the new public school, Carly didn't talk to me about climate change like you would to a child—delicately, sugar-coating it—but as something that was alive and brutal and deadly. She took me to one of her protests. I had never felt so many hearts pounding all at once. Hundreds of thousands of people holding posters with messages like SAVE YOUR ONLY HOME and ONE EARTH ONE CHANCE and CLIMATE JUSTICE NOW.

With Carly's help, I had made a poster that read:

CLIMATE CHANGE TOOK MY MOTHER

It got some attention, and a journalist even interviewed me. Our demands for change—a path to one hundred percent renewable energy, an end to deforestation, investment in communities affected by poverty and pollution—had an urgency that was palpable. That day, it felt like we could do something. For the first time since my mother died, I felt like there was purpose to my life. But then, after we went home and listened to all the promises and all the loopholes and all the barriers, nothing changed.

Carly kept me for three years. Then she got a job—something to do with the recurring wildfires—that required her to travel all over the country, and she said she couldn't adopt me because she couldn't give me the stability I needed. I laughed this off, like when you don't want something to be true. She wrote down her number and email address in my journal and told me I could call her anytime. I wouldn't talk about it or think about it until the social worker came to pick me up, and then I held on to Carly until the social worker had to pry me away.

I was sent to another home, where I was careful not to get attached. That year, I moved three times; I didn't even bother unpacking. I had just been placed with this couple. There was nothing wrong with them, but that very same day, I found blood in my underwear for the first time, so the first discussion I had to have with these new people was about periods. There is nothing comforting about having to ask strangers for sanitary napkins when you have no idea what is happening to your body.

Then I was with the Chomskys for almost a year. The Chomskys were really nice, but they had five kids—six, including me—and a house that was only a little bigger than Carly's. Every Friday, the eight of us would go to McDonald's and I would yell, "My treat!" and tell Mrs. Chomsky to use my money—the money they got from the state to keep me—and we would laugh hard because we all knew how little that was.

The oldest Chomsky kid was Rickie, who was eighteen then. Rickie was always good to me, and I never saw him get into a fight or anything like that. It happened so quick. One day, we heard that he might be doing cocaine, and the next day he was arrested. After that, the Chomskys were in bad shape, what with having to pay the lawyer and everything. They didn't have anything left to give me.

Next, I got assigned to a new caseworker. She was one of those "well-meaning" people who have the opposite effect. My file held consistent feedback from most of the homes: I didn't enjoy nature; I was cynical and difficult to deal with; I was bad at math (which came as a shock, considering the colour of my skin). The caseworker wove these things into conversation, pretending they had come up completely by chance. She talked about faith and God and random acts of nature and how no one is to blame. How kids tend to blame themselves, and how faith will save you. I was so embarrassed for her.

Did I blame myself for swimming away, leaving my mother to die? Or did I blame people like the president for the hurricane that killed my mother? Sometimes two conflicting things can be true at the same time, and there is nothing you can do about it.

My caseworker was determined to give me a better life. Soon, I was placed with this family in a mansion in one of those neighbourhoods with big white houses and long, loopy driveways. The house was large and empty and white. It left me with a cold feeling. Suddenly, I missed Carly's small, colourful, cozy home, where my knees were always bumping into the furniture. The mother, who insisted I call her "Mommy," like her two little boys did, was a realtor, so she was always dressed like a blazer model, one of her hands coiled around what she called her "briefcase-tote." The kids had a nanny and went to a private school. They sent me to the local public school and said they might consider sending me to the private school the following school year. The mother was nice to me in the same way she was nice to her clients. When she didn't want to deal with me, she would say, "Why don't we circle back to that later?"

The father had a very important job. "CEO of a think tank" is what he told me. They had four garages and three cars. He drove a shiny blue car with a jumping horse logo.

I quickly realized that whatever problem I had, he would immediately get rid of it. It was the closest I had felt to love in a long time. If I made a casual statement that I kept losing my pen, he would take out his phone and a package with a ridiculous number of pens would arrive at our doorstep that evening. Once, I saw this ad for an instant camera and I mentioned it at dinner, and that weekend, that exact same camera in the same colour appeared in my room. He bought me a phone with data the second week I lived there.

Unlike all the other homes I had known, this one had a generator that kicked in when we lost power during a storm. The lights would come back on immediately, as if offering us a new life because we were special.

Then, one weekend a few months into my stay, a crew with cameras and big umbrella lights came to the house. They were doing a profile of the father for some business magazine. They took pictures of the family and put me in all the pictures, too. We must have looked ridiculous—a sea of egrets, with a crow in the middle. They even took a picture with just him and me. I was made to sit at the piano and pretend to play (I had never touched a piano before), and he stood behind me watching, his arms folded.

I was certain they were going to adopt me.

That evening, we were in the living room playing Jenga. I had set up the tower, all eighteen rows. I asked him what a think tank did.

"Well, there are all kinds of think tanks—they do research, publish articles, that kind of stuff," he said. "My company conducts strategic analyses of political, economic, and environmental issues."

My interest started to wane, but then he said, "Oil companies hire us to do studies and generate reports that will support their business. For example, new oil reserves have been found here in the US, but government policies prevent oil companies from drilling because of all the pro-climate legislation." His eyebrows jumped. "So if we release a report citing studies we've done that weaken the link between emissions and climate change, they'll have a better chance at being allowed to drill at the new location. We use our influence on media and policy-makers to help change the rules." He placed the last block of row twenty.

"You lie about it?"

"If *we* don't do it, someone else will. There's so much money to be made, you have to decide if you want to make some of it." He paused. "And *that* is how you build a bunker to safeguard yourself and your family from all these storms."

I didn't know what to say. I removed a middle block, and the tower began to wobble.

He continued, "We're pitching to one of the largest oil exporters in the country. If we win this bid, it will take our business to the next level." He stared off for a moment, then smiled. "That's why we did the photo shoot today. To make sure we come across as *good* people, you know?"

The walls around me started closing in, and I tried to focus on finding the next block.

"Come on," he said, "you've seen the world. People don't do good things just from the goodness of their hearts. There's always an agenda."

I nodded, as if I knew this all along.

"All these protests have been hurting the oil business, so those in charge want to associate themselves with companies that are doing good for people, for the environment," he explained. "They need us as much as we need them. I mean, companies like us, and of course, I want that to be *my* company."

My mother's face—swollen and sullied—appeared in my mind. I made my next move, and the tower fell.

The next morning, I called the cops and reported what I thought was the illegal nature of the father's business. The man on the phone tried not to chuckle when he told me that if they could arrest people for stuff like that, half of America would be in prison.

Then I called the Chomskys to find Rickie, but he was in prison again. He had gotten out but was back in because, according to Mrs. Chomsky, "he was at the wrong party at the wrong time." I got in touch with one of Rickie's friends and bought a sandwich bag of cocaine that I paid for with a watch I stole from the father. His big pitch was due in a few days.

I hid the cocaine under the seat in the father's shiny blue car and called the cops from a pay phone. They would never suspect a fourteen-year-old foster child. Like clockwork, they arrived and arrested him. I put on a good show of crying an appropriate amount. He sure didn't pitch anything to anyone, and the story, along with the name of his company, was all over the news.

Soon after this, the mother sent me back. I am in my fourth home this year—an apartment the size of the last family's living room, back in the old, hot, cramped neighbourhood I used to live in with my parents. It has been raining for three days straight—outside the window, in the alleyways, on the streets. This city wasn't built for this type of rain, my mother used to say. The president will need to give a speech soon. Cars are stranded in rising water like floating hippopotamus heads. A group of people wade through the waist-high water, their torsos swinging side to side. It occurs to me that, like everyone else, I have only one home.

Bow Wow

THE SUN IS LOW. A bullseye at the edge of the city. Prithvi stands up from the table and stretches, his cotton kurta crumpled and creased from sitting. His eyes dart across the rooftop restaurant. His silver tresses extend beyond his shoulders, contrasting against the red of his kurta. Years of striving have softened his once-angular face. He untangles his wife's dupatta from her wheelchair. Meera is staring ahead, her eyes blank. Her curls are almost completely grey.

A waiter approaches. "Sir, the food is all ready. Shall we start?" he asks, pointing to the buffet laid out in the centre of the restaurant.

Prithvi spreads out all ten fingers and says, "Ten minutes. Big Brother has yet to arrive."

"Buffet again?" Prithvi's teenaged daughter, Radha, says. "Why can't we ever do à la carte?"

"There's a green smudge on your face," Prithvi's brother-in-law, Mahesh, says. "Side of your forehead."

Prithvi performed Kathakali at the Kowdiar Krishna temple last night, wearing the tall headdress and the umbrella skirt, his lips scarlet and his face the green of paddy fields. He was playing Arjuna, torn between going to war with his family and withdrawing from the battle. Between fulfilling his dharma and renouncing his duty.

"Well, Kathakali isn't going to dance itself," Radha says and chuckles.

"Radha, go downstairs and see if Big Brother is here," Prithvi says.

Earlier, when they arrived at the hotel, the elevator wasn't working, and they waited in the lobby for thirty minutes. The hotel has lost the glory it had during the days when Prithvi's father ran it. Once a five-star hotel, now it is barely three, its walls sagging, overshadowed by younger, taller, swankier hotels around it. When Prithvi was young, he received an overt kind of respect for no reason other than being his father's son. Now, as a renowned playwright, Kathakali artist, and founder of an award-winning theatre group, he doesn't get nearly as much respect in most circles. Big Brother was always their father's favourite—the namesake of the hotel—and had been groomed to take over from him. Prithvi was steadfast in his decision to become a playwright. His father was also steadfast. Playwright, one. Inheritance, zero.

"Yes, Kathakali as an art form would cease to exist if not for your father," Mahesh says.

"Radha, what did I tell you?" Prithvi says to his daughter. "Go check if Big Brother is here."

Radha rolls her eyes. "Uncle knows his way around *his* hotel to *his* rooftop restaurant," she says. Big Brother is God to her because he has promised to send her to California to live with his wife's relatives for her undergraduate degree.

Prithvi is used to people treating him like this, even his daughter. Respect arises from the jobs you hold. Indian Administrative Service officers, air force and army officers, and doctors rank the highest, followed by lawyers, engineers, and government employees. Teachers and nurses rank lower. If you work outside the country, that brings status, too. America, Canada, and England bring more status than the Middle East. If you are an artist, unless you are a celebrity people look down on you because of what they imagine artmaking is like—a frivolous thing to waste your life doing.

Prithvi is accustomed to his extended family celebrating their every little success—promotions, new job offers, salary raises—even when the acclaim for his plays, the recognition of his drama school in a national newspaper, the prestigious awards he has won for his contributions to the art world go uncelebrated.

Mahesh has a government job, a senior position, which

gives him the right to offer unsolicited advice at all times. He has two sons; the younger one is studying to become a lawyer, and the older one and his wife are expecting their second child.

"Your drama school was going pretty well, no? Why this Kathakali and all?" Mahesh says.

Prithvi's wife, Meera, knew what to do with Mahesh when he got like this. She never raised her voice but found a way to rebuke her brother and the rest of her family for not giving Prithvi the respect he deserved. She would say things like, "Prithvi doesn't need titles to feel like a man, unlike other people around here." She was the only one who could silence Mahesh. But Meera doesn't speak anymore. She is relearning how to use her vocal cords. The doctors say it's a miracle she's out of the coma after being mangled like that under the bus.

When Prithvi got the call from the hospital, he wasn't surprised. Meera drove her Kinetic Honda scooter at speeds it wasn't meant to go. When he sat behind her as she drove him around, he was scared for his life. She was perennially in a hurry. She worked full time at the elementary school and part time at the dance institute. Prithvi used to wonder if those things gave her a thrill—rushing, being barely on time, dashing through slivers between trucks. The near-escapes.

The crash, however, wasn't her fault. Two pedestrians and a beggar at the roundabout confirmed that the bus had lost control and jammed into her.

"Stop bothering him," Sneha says. She is Mahesh's wife, perhaps the only one in the family aside from Meera who respects Prithvi.

"Well, things would have been different," Mahesh says. "That's all I'm saying."

"Different for whom?" Prithvi says.

"For my sister, who else?"

Déjà vu. Prithvi feels like he's newly married again and has just told his family he's walking away from his inheritance to become a full-time playwright and run his own drama school.

They were at Mahesh and Sneha's new home on Gandhi Nagar. Mahesh was in a bad mood already, something to do with his neighbours. He said he didn't know when they moved in that the house next door was occupied by prostitutes. Mahesh was in his early thirties and had a lot of rage. As the oldest of three children, he had taken on the responsibility of being the man of the house after his father died when he was just sixteen.

"How dare they walk around like that on the terrace?" Mahesh said. "We are a civilized society."

"Walk around like what?" Meera asked.

"Naked!" Mahesh said. "Not wearing anything. Zilch."

Meera giggled, her eyes flashing mischievously. "Where?"

"Rooftop! She was hanging damp clothes on the clothesline, her backside completely bare."

"Well, maybe that's because she didn't have any clean clothes to wear," Sneha said and laughed, slapping the table.

"Shut up, Sneha," Mahesh said. "I wrote a letter to the association. This has to end! I will not live next to whores."

Mahesh spoke with so much righteousness it made Prithvi cringe. Meera should have picked another time to break the news to her brother that her husband had just walked away from millions to start his own drama school. The one thing Mahesh felt he had control over in those days was his sister's life. He had arranged for Meera to meet Prithvi, the heir of the Raj Palace. He invited his boss and his colleagues and threw a grand wedding, spending all the money he had saved specifically for this purpose. His little sister was the greatest responsibility of his life.

Mahesh did not take the news well. Sweat droplets accumulated on his already balding head. He raised his voice to Prithvi for the first time: "Why do you think we married Meera off to you?"

"You didn't marry me off. I married Prithvi of my own free will," Meera said. "Because he has talent. And vision. And faith in himself."

For months, Mahesh tried to talk Prithvi out of his decision, reminding him repeatedly how ridiculous it was to walk away from money like that. He told Prithvi he could work in the family business and write plays as a hobby. At one point, he even tried to convince Meera to leave Prithvi.

Prithvi had learned that arguing with family, or anyone outside the world of the performing arts, was futile. They were never going to understand his passion and the strides he had made in the theatre scene in Kerala. They were never going to understand the thrill he felt when he stood on a stage and bared himself raw. That succulent moment of truth when there were no barriers between him and his audience. When Prithvi took his theatre troupe to festivals around the world, Mahesh used to say it was an excuse for him to kiss white people with no morals.

The waiter comes by to refill their drinks. "Shall we start?" he asks.

"Yes, I'm starving," Radha says.

"Let me try Big Brother," Prithvi says, his phone to his ear. Big Brother, always in impeccable suits, his hair dyed black, going from one important meeting to another.

The rooftop restaurant is the only thing in the hotel that has aged well: the red tiles, the ornamental lampposts, the view of the city on one side and the forest on the other, the varieties of hibiscus plants lining the perimeter. They've booked the entire establishment for the celebration—Prithvi and Meera's twenty-fifth wedding anniversary. More than seventy people have gathered here, and Big Brother is paying for it.

"Big Brother's going to be late. Let's start," Prithvi says, ending the unanswered call.

Meera used to sing. It is her voice Prithvi misses the most. She was also a Bharatanatyam dancer. After Meera graduated from college, her mother told her that dancing after a certain age was for women with loose bodies and looser morals. She told her to get married instead.

When Prithvi first came to see Meera at her family home, she was the only one who wasn't in awe of his father's hotel legacy. While her mother and brothers were pandering to his father and Big Brother, Meera asked Prithvi if he knew how to make round chapatis, which Prithvi found refreshing. He had already met a few girls by then, and they all advertised their cooking prowess. Prithvi told Meera that he didn't, but he would learn how to make chapatis before the wedding.

Prithvi brings Meera a plate of food from the buffet—fried rice, cucumber raita—and helps her eat.

Meera's mother has just arrived. "Sorry, so much traffic," she says. "How are you, my little one?" Her eyes tear up instantly.

Meera nods and gestures for her mother to eat by bringing her puckered hand to her mouth.

"I'll eat after you. I can help you," her mother says.

"No, Amma, you go get food," Prithvi says. "I'll help her."

Meera eats slowly, bringing one careful spoonful after another to her mouth. Her mother piles a plate with food—fried rice, raita, paneer masala, masala dosa, chutney, poori, butter chicken, everything touching everything else.

Prithvi wipes yogourt from the corners of Meera's lips. Her mother sighs and says, "Who would have thought of all people Meera would be the one who needs help eating?"

"She's doing much better," Prithvi says. "She got ready today almost all by herself."

"Is that enough food for her?" Meera's mother asks, eyeing Meera's plate.

"She doesn't need much food, Amma. Her doctor told us to be careful how much she eats and what she eats, especially because she doesn't get much exercise."

Mahesh shakes his empty glass at the waiter, gesturing for more whiskey. So far, Mahesh and his mother have successfully ignored each other.

"I'm still amazed by how you take care of her," Meera's mother says. "You haven't travelled in so long. If you need any help, let me know. I'm always here."

This type of pity and empty promise doesn't affect Prithvi much anymore. Meera's mother has visited her daughter only five times in the four years since her accident. After Prithvi made it clear that he was not giving up control of the money Meera had received from the insurance company, her mother disappeared.

"I'm definitely calling you the next time I need help," Prithvi says with exaggerated enthusiasm.

"Anything except taking her to the bathroom or giving her a shower or taking her for doctor visits. That I can't do," Meera's mother says, in between bites. "You know my knees are bad." She spreads a glob of ketchup over her poori, like that is something normal to do. She doesn't even know that Meera can't go to the bathroom. She hasn't noticed the bag hanging beside her daughter's wheelchair. She continues, "I may not have said this to you earlier, but Meera is lucky to have married you."

Mahesh laughs at this. "People around here have a short memory," he says.

Mahesh hasn't spoken to his mother in seventeen years because she picked the wrong side in an argument between him and his brother. His brother wanted to use the money he had received from their father's will to invest in a pyramid scheme. Mahesh said it was a ridiculous idea and he would lose all the money (which he eventually did). But his mother supported her youngest, protecting him from her oldest. The entire extended family took sides, some supporting Mahesh and others agreeing with his mother and brother.

His mother mutters something under her breath, then straightens her spine. She sticks her nose up and rests her spoon on her plate. "You turned out to be a better husband and a better son than most," she says to Prithvi. "Despite not having a real job, you managed everything so well. I hope your brother is helping you somewhat."

Prithvi doesn't try to convince people that being a playwright is a real job. Yet the woman is right. If not for Big Brother and the enormous insurance cheque, Prithvi would never have been able to afford the kind of treatments Meera needed. The surgeries, the extensive therapy, the medicines, the medical equipment at home.

"Yeah, best husband ever. Has everyone forgotten Juliana?" Mahesh says, slurring his words. He gets like this every time he drinks and has barely any memory of his behaviour when he sobers up.

"That's enough," Sneha says, trying to take Mahesh's glass of whiskey away. He pulls it back from her.

Prithvi hasn't thought about Juliana in ages. The skinny girl from Sweden who was a student at his drama school. Meera and Prithvi welcomed her into their home, and she lived with them during the three years she was training in Kerala. She found her calling there, shining in the role of Hidimbi. Everyone knew she wanted to fuck Prithvi; there was electricity in the air when they were together. The way she carried herself around him, the way she found reasons to touch him, the tone of her voice when she spoke to him. Her desire, so green and bare.

He would have been disappointed if she hadn't been attracted to him. They did spend a lot of time together. And he had that effect on women. His hair, his personality, his command of his craft. He was always hyper-aware of the attention. And he did his fair share of flirting, too. Subtle, but he knew what he was doing. It was good for his art, he used to say. When he and Meera were young, it bothered her. When he toured, he didn't wear his wedding ring. "It doesn't suit the characters I play," he used to tell her. As they grew older, she seemed to get used to it. Or perhaps she stopped caring.

Sometimes it amazes Prithvi that they've made it this far. As supportive as Meera had been, she used to bristle at Prithvi. For being away from home for long stretches. For being too close to his female actors. For leaving the child-rearing entirely to her. At the time, Prithvi made no effort to make her feel special.

Now he is consumed by guilt, thinking of the ways he strayed. All the times he lied and she knew he was lying. Meera used to say, "You're a bad liar, you know that, right?" He didn't expect to feel this way now, but seeing his wife like this, so helpless, has changed him. She looks like a different person now. Before the accident, her hair was always dyed black, her feet fast, and her eyes lined with kajal.

"Travelling to Europe together. Sharing rooms!" Mahesh is still rambling. "All that is forgiven now?"

Prithvi doesn't bother to confront his brother-in-law. He looks at Meera to see how she's reacting. She sees him watching her and smiles. Perhaps even chuckles.

Sneha manages to take Mahesh's drink away. Prithvi

wipes Meera's mouth with a damp napkin and wheels her away toward the side of the roof overlooking the forest. The sky is purple now.

Mahesh's granddaughter, who is five, hops sideways toward them. "Can I push the wheely-chair?" Her pigtails are tight resting over the Peter Pan collar of her dress.

Prithvi says, "It's too heavy for you, Malu."

"Why does she need this chair?"

"She had an accident, remember? She's still getting better. She can't walk yet."

"Can she talk?"

"A few words, yes. But she's still learning," Prithvi says gently. "Like you were learning to talk a few years ago." He finds a video on his phone of Meera singing, not long before the accident. "See? She used to sing like this," he says.

In the video, Meera is wearing a Kanchipuram silk saree, her greys barely visible. Kajal accentuates her eyes. She is singing a devotional song about Lord Krishna revealing his Vishwaroop—his immortal, all-encompassing self—to Arjuna, reminding him to do his duty. Her voice is raw honey.

Malu watches the video and then examines Meera. She is at eye level with her in her wheelchair.

"Let me try Big Brother again," Prithvi says.

Meera smiles at Malu. The light from a lamppost casts a shadow of the wheelchair on the floor. Meera wraps her right hand around her left palm, sticking out her pinky and thumbs. The shadow of her clasped hands looks like an alien dog.

"Bow wow," she says to Malu.

Singing for the Gods

PKOC LALITHA SINGS WITH her eyes pinched into the microphone at the Ganesh Temple of Santa Clara in front of about a hundred people—devotees, so to speak—also with their eyes closed, mesmerized by her voice. We are sitting behind her on the stage, criss-cross applesauce, wondering if she will ever falter. She sits in her chair, this plastic throne-like thing, her back facing us, her right hand tapping her lap, counting the musical measures. Her hair is tied into a bun, and around it she has arranged a jasmine flower garland, her curly grey fly-aways making a halo around her head against the glaring fluorescent lights. Beside her, Siddharth plays the tabla and Sujatha the veena, microphones pointing down to the instruments as if bowing to them.

PKOC Lalitha gets her name from Pravasi Keralites of California, which is the association she founded in the 1980s to bring together Malayalees in Northern California. People began to call her P.K.O.C. Lalitha back then to distinguish her from all the other Lalithas they knew. We shortened it to PKOC, pronouncing it "peacock," which is really more appropriate, considering how she struts into the temple in her showy best—stiff Kanchipuram sarees, flowers in her hair, heavy gold jimikkis stretching her earlobes.

For years, PKOC Lalitha has been training us to sing like her—or, as she puts it, "sing so that Lord Krishna will pause and listen." She has us memorize songs in Sanskrit that we don't understand, and when we stumble she says, "Lord Krishna will die of a heart attack if he hears this."

Radha, new to the US at the time, replied, "How will Krishna die? Isn't he God?"

"You have no respect for the kala," PKOC responded. "That's why the kala refuses you."

Radha came from money—her family owned a hotel back in Kerala—but here she lived with her aunt's relatives and quickly realized that she didn't have the freedom to be who she used to be back in her hometown. Like us, all she had here was the music.

PKOC has her music students touch her feet one by one, before and after practice, as if she holds the key to the music and she'll open the door, bit by bit, if we respect her enough.

Now that PKOC is seventy-eight, her voice resembles that of M. S. Subbulakshmi, the legend from India whose devotional songs fill the mornings of every South Indian Brahmin household in our neighbourhood, especially her devotional *Bhaja Govindam*, which is what PKOC is singing now. But PKOC compares herself to the "Nightingale of India," Lata Mangeshkar, and even goes a step further, saying that her voice is superior to Mangeshkar's.

"Lata sold herself to Bollywood," she says, like they were old friends. "The reason I am sitting here, teaching you bunch of lazy fools, and not being honoured by the president of India, is because I have devoted myself to Lord Krishna. Or else I'd have given Lata a run for her money."

PKOC's claim is never contested, so she goes on. "Have you noticed how much her voice has deteriorated as she has aged? But she still sings for these bony bimbos dancing in the rain with exposed midriffs. I could *never* do that with my talent."

Toward the end of the song, we join the chorus, the microphone placed high above us so our adolescent voices don't overpower PKOC's. Still, Sujatha's voice rises through the speakers, the vibrations merging with PKOC's.

After the performance, PKOC announces that she will be retiring soon from singing at the temple and teaching us music, and she will be appointing a successor. Devotees protest—they cannot imagine someone else taking over the space she has occupied for over thirty years. During PKOC's reign, several greying ammoomas have vied for her position of power at the temple and in the local Brahmin community, but we know that she has decided on Sujatha, her protege.

Sujatha, at twenty-three, is the oldest among the students, the youngest being ten. Unlike most of us, she was born with a phenomenal vocal range. The only one among us who belongs to the Namboothiri caste—the "purest of pure" Brahmins from Kerala, according to PKOC—she had trained with a guru since the age of three. After she moved here at age thirteen, she continued her practice with PKOC, growing, glowing, in that way only music can transform a person.

As for us, you could say we are held here by our only talent—singing. We fail miserably at the STEM courses our Bay Area parents think we should excel at. We don't blend in at our schools, in our American communities, so we go the other way, stubbornly sticking to our otherness, our Malayali-ness, and to the one thing we are actually good at. Our hair oily and braided, proudly walking into our classrooms with our jackets smelling of asafetida and trapped masala, deaf to the voices that say, "What's that disgusting smell?" we are masters of not fitting in. Not for a moment do we let shame pierce our skins. For we are secure in the knowledge that, here at the temple, we have our place. When we sing, whether Lord Krishna listens or not, we can feel the hearts beating in the temple, enthralled by our voices, like we are divinity embodied in scrawny little brown bodies.

. . .

Every full-moon night, the temple performs Satya Narayana puja for sponsors who want to be blessed by good fortune—career, money, family, the works. The puja is an all-inclusive ritual, unlike, say, the Ganapathi homam, a specific one that is meant to remove obstacles before you start something new, like buying a new home. The Satya Narayana puja is the one-stop shop of pujas. And it wasn't an original feature of the temple when it was exclusively a Kerala temple. A few years ago, the management realized they couldn't compete with the grand North Indian temples in Malibu and BAPS Swaminarayan Mandir in LA by catering just to Malayalis, so they rebranded as a generic South Indian temple, changing the name from Santa Clara Krishnan Kovil to Ganesh Temple of Santa Clara. Originally located in a small space, with just a Krishna and Ganesh altar, the temple was rebuilt, renovated, and expanded. Several new altars were created: Tirupati for the Telugus, Goddess Lakshmi for the Kannadigas, Shiva-Parvati-Nataraj for the Tamils, Sita-Ram-Hanuman for the North Indians. For good measure, they also added Durga and Navagraha.

The icing on the cake was the Satya Narayana altar.

This March, the full moon—pink moon, this time—falls on a Saturday. Weekend Satya Narayana pujas always teem with devotees. The shoe racks at the entrance overflow with the footwear everybody takes off as a sign of respect for the gods. Most of the sponsors pay for the whole year, knowing their names and nakshatras—the celestial houses representing who they are on this earth—will be included in the chanting each month. The temple has gone to great lengths to assure the devotees that the benefits are the same whether they attend or not, so as not to affect the temple's bottom line. Still, on a weekend, the devotees show up in their temple best. They pay seven hundred dollars per family for the year, which is peanuts for these double-salaried STEM households. And the puja only helps grow their riches, so it's a win-win.

PKOC sits on her plastic throne beside the altar with a notebook on her lap, issuing instructions to the pujari, a small man with a cabbage face and a half-bald head. Steel plates of prasadam—cashews, almonds, pistachios, raisins, dates, dried pineapple, even warm homemade kesari, that semolina dessert we can't get enough of—rest on the floor in front of the altar. We are seated on mats beside PKOC as devotees spread out mat after mat, looking at one another, bowing to PKOC, making their presence known.

Sujatha shows up late in a pink Kanchipuram, with a man we have never seen before. Medium build, clean shaven, rectangular, ash-brown face. He is wearing a Tommy Hilfiger red and blue checkered shirt with a mundu. When he sits down on the mat beside Sujatha, we can see that he doesn't have confidence in the mundu and wears pants underneath the fabric wrapped around his waist. They sit far from the altar, which is all the seating that's left when you're this late.

PKOC leans toward us and says, "What is Sujatha doing with this Pulayan boy?"

PKOC has accused him of being of the lowest caste—a Dalit—and we know that, with her sources, she is probably right, but we don't want to risk a confrontation so we busy ourselves distributing the glossy Satya Narayana katha booklets to the devotees.

The pujari's lips are moving like a mouse's, his chants mere mutters. Now and then, he raises his brass Aarti lamp with thirty-two balls of fire toward us, and everyone bows, closing their eyes, saying quick prayers. We watch PKOC watching Sujatha, picturing the circuits in her brain lighting up as the wrinkles around her eyes converge.

After the chanting, it is time to read the Satya Narayana katha. Anyone can volunteer to read this text translated into English, which gives each event a wild, unpredictable quality. One month, we could have an aging appuppan holding on to the microphone like a long-lost artifact; another month, we could be subjected to a young child thrust forward by eager parents, taking forever; another time, we could listen to a fast reader, swallowing words, racing through the thing, which is what we prefer. Today, a new family—new to the temple, that is—sends their six-year-old to the stage. His mouth moves in slow motion, sounding out words one at a time. He does not care for punctuation and stops where the line stops, not at the periods. We can feel the collective headache everyone in the temple is suffering except the kid and his parents. He's the only thing standing between us and all that prasadam we can see and smell. We are rolling our eyes, hoping PKOC will put an end to this torture, but she is staring intently at Sujatha and her friend, who are looking at each other with soft eyes, giggling.

Finally, at the end of the third story, PKOC takes charge. Looking at us, she says, "Let's give an opportunity to someone else now." Five of us spring up and run to the microphone. We take turns speed-reading the rest of the stories. In a few short minutes, we prostrate ourselves, then get up to distribute and accept prasadam.

Sujatha is walking around, seemingly oblivious of PKOC's watchful eye, her friend by her side, both of them holding plates of dried fruit, nuts, and kesari. She introduces him to everyone as her fiancé.

When they reach PKOC, the man extends his free hand and says, "Hello, I am Girish."

We hold our breath as his hand hangs in the air in front of PKOC, who clasps her own hands behind her back. "Girish what?" she says.

He retracts his hand and says, "Girish Velayudhan." The poor man has no idea what he has just given away.

PKOC looks at us with her *What did I tell you?* expression—eyes beady, lips pinched toward one side. We look away, at the ceiling, at our fingernails, at the milk flowing down Ganesha.

Later, we learn that PKOC has given Sujatha an ultimatum: call off the wedding, or PKOC will give Sujatha's coveted position to someone else.

We try to talk to PKOC after her fury has subsided. We point out that nobody cares about caste anymore. Especially here in the US.

"Since when are you people PhDs in this matter?" She looks at us with disapproving eyes, like we're a swarm of something insignificant but provoking, like fruit flies. "Sujatha is a pure Brahmin. How can she marry a Dalit? It's disgraceful!"

We tell her that people have been marrying across caste, even across religion, for ages, Hindus marrying Christians and Muslims, too.

PKOC looks like she is about to slap us. "Let me ask you this. How many big companies are led by Indians or Indian-born Americans?"

We shrug, and then count in our heads. One, two, three, four. Radha says tentatively, "Eight?"

"How many of these CEOS are from lower castes?"

We gasp, first racking our brains thinking of the CEOS'

last names, hoping to prove her wrong, then shocked at the absurdity of engaging with her like this.

We don't want to accept her claim, so we tell her it's probably just a coincidence. What do white people know about Indian castes anyway?

"Who do you think is interviewing all these people? You walk into these company offices, it's all our people. You can never escape your last name. I've been here for forty years, at least give me some credit."

When enough time has passed that it's clear she has made her point, she says, "You think I am just an old lady, stuck in my ways, out of touch with the real world. Once you marry a lower-caste man, you change your last name and that's it, you are screwed."

We are stunned, our hands quiet by our sides. We think about our last names and where they fall on her pyramid—if we are even on the pyramid.

"Well, Sujatha doesn't have to change her last name," Radha says. "And besides, she is a kindergarten teacher, so why are we even talking about this?"

"You think I will pass on my job to her if she marries that lowly man?" PKOC scoffs. "I have cauliflower in my ears, or what?"

• • •

This March is auspicious—two full moons in the same month. The second one falls on the last day of March, a Sunday. Sujatha is indignant, going around telling everyone that PKOC is a bigot, but nobody will listen to anything ill said of her. They have placed her on a pedestal, and they would rather look away than admit any wrongdoing on her part.

PKOC stops showing up for practice. Her knees are failing her, and she has finally gotten herself a motorized wheelchair. We see her moseying around the temple in it, but she ignores us. Sujatha takes over. Whether PKOC is there or not, we are tethered to our practice, the only thing that makes us feel wanted in this searing world. When we are on stage singing, we don't do it for PKOC or Sujatha, we do it for us. This is the one place—in the Bay Area, in the US—where we feel we belong, where everything is the way it is supposed to be.

Sujatha arrives early for the performance that precedes the Satya Narayana puja, wearing her mother's Kanchipuram—a bleeding mustard with a thick gold border. She looks like Goddess Lakshmi herself, her fiancé by her side. She walks through the main entrance, gently holding up her saree so she won't trip over the stair at the threshold. She prays at the Ganesh altar, a gentle smile on her lips. The pujari pours holy water into her cupped palm. She drinks, and then with her pinky, she dabs sandalwood paste on her forehead. Her fiancé copies everything she does, trailing behind her as she circles the altar three times before coming to the stage, where we are all seated.

In no time, PKOC arrives in her wheelchair, driving up the ramp that leads to the side entrance, wearing a saree—we plunge into a state of panic—in the exact same mustard shade and with the same six-inch border as Sujatha's. If there are any differences in the Zari patterns, we can't see them from where we are sitting. After she completes one round of the Ganesh altar, PKOC sees Sujatha and comes charging toward us.

She stops at the foot of the stage, her eyeballs about to pop out into our hands. "At least wear your own saree!" she screams. Then she tries to storm out, but the wheelchair makes it a slow-motion exit.

When PKOC crosses the threshold to the foyer, Sujatha goes after her, and we follow both of them. We stop at a safe distance. The fiancé is smart and stays back with us.

Sujatha steps in front of PKOC and blocks her path. "How long are you going to ignore me?"

PKOC flashes her most disgusted look—lips lopsided, eyes reduced to wrinkled skin.

"You know what your problem is?" Sujatha says. "You're jealous of me. You know I'm better than you, and you can't stand it."

PKOC draws fluid from her lungs and spits at Sujatha, but

because she is seated and Sujatha is standing, it lands on the floor, a blob of translucence on the black tiles.

"See, you just proved what I said," Sujatha says. "You are scared everyone will know I am better than you."

Now PKOC thrusts her wheelchair toward Sujatha, who steps backward just in time.

"Crazy, jealous woman!" Sujatha screams.

PKOC brakes. "If you are so sure about your talent, prove it now, here in front of everyone. Let's find out who is better!" She turns the wheelchair around and heads back inside.

"Fine!" Sujatha says and goes after her.

PKOC gestures to Siddharth to set up the stage. He moves slowly, carefully, toward the middle of the stage, as if he will explode if he rushes. Looking both excited and scared, he sets up the tabla and two microphones. PKOC and Sujatha position themselves almost side by side, PKOC a few inches in front of Sujatha, their silver toe rings sparkling under the stage lights. Siddharth adjusts the microphone for PKOC. Then he sits down, his skinny arms loose around the tabla. As he begins to play, he relaxes a bit. The atmosphere in the hall becomes tense. The three of them look different now, out of our hands, belonging to the devotees.

We stand around the two large speakers by the edge of the stage, feeling Siddharth's beats enter us through our feet. And then we feel PKOC's rich and heavy notes as she sings "Govardhana Girisham." Her face looks troubled, lacking its usual ease. After the Pallavi—the first stanza—she steps back, leaving the air empty as a challenge for Sujatha.

Sujatha closes her eyes and takes over. Her voice is shriller. She doesn't look confident, and we think our hearts are going to split in this clamour to choose between the two of them.

We witness this exchange: PKOC expresses something; Sujatha answers. A roar rises from within each woman, rearranging the air around us as we stand, hypnotized by their mastery. This arrangement of molecules in the air, created by them from scratch, from nothingness—it is as if the gods have finally descended here in Santa Clara. Two yellow suns—one old, one new, both burning brilliantly. We are wrapped in gooseflesh.

They go through song after song, not one note, one word, out of place. PKOC's face begins to show desperation—what, was she expecting Sujatha to fail? After all, she is her protege. Our feet begin to tingle, from standing, from expectation, from all the music entering us.

NOW PKOC delivers the final blow. She starts with the next song, "Vishnu Sahasranamam," and we know this will be the last one. "A Thousand Names of Vishnu" has 108 couplets, and none of us has been able to sing it without glancing at the lyrics. The few times PKOC has tried to make us do it, we have simply gone blank with panic.

Sujatha takes out her phone to look up the lyrics, but PKOC says, "No cheating."

Sujatha's face turns a heavy orange; she is sweating in her saree, her lipstick long gone. She takes over after the introductory Dhyanam section, her eyes focused on a point in the distance, holding on to her memory. We are installed right in front of the stage, mouthing along with her whatever words we know.

After what feels like fifteen minutes, Sujatha's voice drops, and we can barely hear her. She is stuck on the forty fifth couplet, "Rutu-sudar-shanah-kalaa." She tries it again, beginning from the previous couplet, but we know the place she has reached. Nothing is available to her anymore.

PKOC's face contorts into a wild smile, and her laugh comes out of the loudspeakers like an earthquake, crackling, then turns into a series of desperate donkey calls. Siddharth stops playing the tabla and the air fills with PKOC's repugnance.

Sujatha leaves the stage quietly, her face sallow. PKOC calls after her, "You think I am jealous of *you?*"

Our skin crawls for PKOC. For all the eyes that are judging her. We can see the turn, the fall from grace. Her bigotry cannot be ignored because it is public now.

"I've seen lots of girls like you. Coming and going." The rant goes on. "You know how many people know me around here? And how many people know *you?* You are a NOBODY! You are nothing without me. And now with this Dalit boy you insist on marrying, your downfall is complete."

The audience gasps. The pujaris step out of the altars facing the stage, stunned out of their cocoons. The manager of the temple, who has finally heard the commotion from the front desk, runs to turn the speakers off.

PKOC will never make an appearance at the temple again, and when we occasionally bump into her wheeling around the Kerala grocery store or the community centre, she'll nod at us with a distant look and turn away. The sight of her will remind us of all the music she taught us and all the joy it brought us, the memory of a simpler time when we associated her only with music, and we'll run after her and touch her feet, like she always made us do before and after practice.

And then we will leave her and go to Sujatha, who will treat us like equals, irrespective of our last names, which will be jarring at first. This will take some getting used to, but it will make our song sweeter, our voices fuller.

And when Sujatha gets married, we will be in her bridal party, holding the Ashtamangalyam plates of offering filled with gold and rice and Kumkum and the bronze kindi filled with holy water. After a short honeymoon in Key West, she will return to the temple, wearing a salwar kurta instead of a saree, creating an atmosphere of ease. She'll sit in the middle of the stage, Siddharth by her side on the tabla, the veena across her lap, her right elbow resting on the gourd-like resonator. Her husband will watch from the front row, his glow complementing hers. PKOC's old throne, that cheap plastic chair, will sit beside the stage, holding cleaning rags. When Sujatha starts to play, we will close our eyes, and let the vibrations in the air enter us, again.

Bestsellers

THE CERAMICS—POTS, MUGS, FIGURINES—are nothing to be proud of. If someone had told me all those years ago, when my future was bright and everything good was still ahead of me, when the dean of the college told me I was among the "cream of the crop" and destined to make a difference in the world, that I would be selling ceramics for a living, I would have been terribly offended. I never had any creative inclinations, so it was as much a surprise to me as it was to the people who knew me.

I sell them on Instagram, with pictures I snap on my phone. And with every piece I tell a story, a story from my life. My bestseller for six months straight has been a hand-made ceramic figurine of a pouting woman holding out a phone. The description under the image reads:

CeramicsByNilofer: Honey, It's for You!
*I moved to this country for my husband, abandoning my medical
school education back home in India. For me to find a job as a
doctor here would have required years of training and money
we didn't have, so I worked as a receptionist at a dentist's office.
He, however, got promoted every two years at his sales job. He
could be very charming when he wanted to.*
    *In the ten years we were married I fiercely stayed the same,
and he became unrecognizable. When we were first together, he
used to say that couples who used terms of endearment for each
other were phonies. Now he's gone and found himself a woman
who picks up the phone when I call and says, "Honey, it's for you!"*
    I designed this piece in her honour.
    Who wants one? To order, go to my website.

The word "designed" is a stretch. The phone is dispro-
portionate, the figurine's face is smudgy, and her eyes
remain unrealistically shut because I don't know how to
make eyeballs. I can never make two pieces look the same,
but that is part of their one-of-a-kind charm. And for the
price of a figurine, my customers also get a story. It's the
story that moves people. I have found that people will gladly
spend money simply to feel something. This type of blatant
pity party goes against everything I stood for—my parents
raised me and my four sisters to tuck away our problems
into secret compartments, never to be opened.

The hardest part was leaving the home I shared with my husband. It had a red door, beautiful vaulted ceilings, and shiny hardwood floors that I polished for years. It was difficult for me to accept that I would lose this home, as if it weren't just a home but a proxy for what our marriage could have been.

I moved into a boxy basement apartment within walking distance of the dental office. In the winter, snow accumulated in the window wells and blocked the two small windows. This house was at least a hundred years old, and the basement smelled like days-old broccoli soup left inside a smoker's car. The washroom was so small that if I didn't close the standing shower door, I couldn't close the bathroom door. I told no one about the move except my parents back in Hyderabad. It seemed like I had stepped on a long rickety bridge, and I had no idea where it would take me. I thought my parents would be on the next flight to Toronto, but they told me that I was being selfish and foolish—the two inexcusable sins in our family. They found my situation too shameful to share with people. I didn't blame them. They were the ones surrounded by all our relatives, forced to go to all the family events, while I could hide here in the basement.

The laundry room was on the landing between the basement and the first floor, where the landlady lived. On sunny days when she did her laundry, I would return from my morning walk and the snow would glisten like diamonds, and pillows of steam would rise from the vent like baby ghosts.

The landlady was a single mom with two little children. She had a finance job, the kind my parents would have approved of. But all I heard her do was plead with her kids and cry herself to sleep. The kids threw tantrums regularly, banging doors shut or throwing themselves on the floor and screaming. And she would say things like, "Sweetie, please don't do that," or "Honey, do you want to sit in the corner and think about your choices?" If I had behaved that way when I was a kid, my mother would have whacked my face. My landlady had the kids with her all the time except on alternate weekends, so I doubted that she got any time to herself. I felt grateful I'd never had kids, though I wanted them so badly once.

Another bestseller in my store is a hand-moulded figurine of twin babies sleeping on a blanket. Their heads are big and their hands and legs are splayed out, like startled clowns. The description under the picture reads:

CeramicsByNilofer: We're Having Twins!
For as long as I can remember, I wanted to have kids. I am one of five girls, and I wanted to have five girls of my own. Before I married my husband, he wanted to have kids, too. But whenever I broached the topic, he said he wasn't ready.

Ten years went by, and I was in my midthirties when my

husband asked for a divorce. A year later, I saw a photo of him on Facebook, his arms wrapped around his new wife, his chin resting in her ash-blond hair.

"We're having twins!" the caption read.

I designed this piece the day I saw that Facebook post. My ceramics are my babies now. And I love them a lot.

Do you love them, too? To order, go to my website.

• • •

The story of how I came to create these things seems worth telling. During the divorce proceedings, watching pottery videos on Instagram became a daily distraction. Like smoking or stress-eating—an escape from the unbearable present moment. Time-lapse reels of talented hands throwing stiff balls of clay onto the potter's wheel, pulling and shaping them into mugs, bowls, vases, or anything those hands desired, offered hope that someday I might be able to control my life in the same way.

Every time I got an email from my ex's lawyer, my entire body would go into shock. His lawyer was a female version of him. She had the same eyes—distant, cold, and piercing. She wasn't supposed to copy me on her emails to my lawyer; she did it as an intimidation tactic. As I read and reread the caustic legalese, I would feel out of breath and my chest hurt like I was about to die.

But it happened so many times that I realized I wasn't going to die, and somehow that seemed even worse. Then I would have to drink a glass of water and take deep breaths. The rest of the day would be a wash. I'd lie in bed, scrolling through more pottery videos. I would like and comment on every video I watched: *I did not see that coming*; *You outdid yourself here*; or *Where can I buy one??*

In those days, so much of my time went into watching pottery reels that I started to dream I was spinning on a massive potter's wheel inside large blobs of clay, my body stretching and submitting to the wheel.

In my new neighbourhood, I didn't know anyone except the landlady and this woman named Rahel. I had met Rahel at the dental office when she came in for a cleaning. She must have been in her fifties, but if I hadn't seen her file, I wouldn't have guessed it. It was the way she carried herself, like she was just getting started, like she completely believed that life was *for* her, that gave her a never-aging look. She wore a perfume that reminded me of my grandmother's talcum powder. And she treated me with a curious affection, like a parent who hadn't seen their child in years. Rahel often visited a florist near the dental office, and she would stop by on her way there and chat with me if I wasn't busy. Once, I house-sat for her, and

I loved her home—a Victorian townhouse near Trinity Bellwoods filled with artwork and souvenirs collected from her travels. She lived alone and was happier than most people I'd met.

One day I ran into Rahel at Food Basics and she said, "I was thinking about you, Nilofer." This struck me as odd because nobody thinks about me for no reason, and I wondered if she wanted me to house-sit for her again. But to my surprise, she said, "I was going to take pottery lessons, and for some reason I thought you'd be interested." She smiled with astonishing brightness.

I saw this as a sign. *How* could this person I'd known for less than a year know of my private obsession?

My eyes stung and the dairy aisle spun around me. I felt like I was going to burst, like I was at the edge of something. Involuntarily, my arms wrapped themselves around Rahel. "Oh my God, yes," I said. "Absolutely."

I couldn't really afford pottery lessons, but I figured I could manage it if I delayed paying my lawyer by a few months. He was a good guy, which made him a bad lawyer, I found out later. Rahel and I registered for Introduction to Pottery at the city-run pottery studio on Fridays at 7 p.m. The two weeks I spent waiting for classes to start were the happiest time of my life in years. I imagined my hands moving expertly, turning blocks of clay into exquisite works of art, giving meaning to the earth, and to myself.

. . .

On our first day of class, Rahel met me outside the pottery studio and we walked in together. The room was large and almost completely brown. It smelled like earth. Three students were already seated on stools around a large table at the centre of the room. We were greeted by the instructor, Brian, a tall man with large hands. He asked us to pick up a bag of clay each from a shelf marked FRIDAYS and showed us how to cut the clay using string. He spent the whole class teaching us how to prepare the clay. This involved a process called wedging, which he insisted was not kneading, although that's what it looked like to me.

"Kneading would lead to bubbles, but here we are wedging," said Brian. "Draw the clay toward you, and then push it down from the sides, never from the middle."

He told us to do this to our piece of clay several times, and then to cut it using our string to check if there were any bubbles. The other students, including Rahel, looked like they had been wedging clay since they were toddlers, while I barely had the upper body strength to press down on it.

Brian walked around the table observing and answering questions. When he came to me and saw my block of clay, unchanged, he said, "Show me your hands."

I extended my hands. Dried clay coated my cuticles and was stuck underneath my fingernails.

Brian flipped my hands over, looked at my palms, and said, "Smallest adult hands I've ever seen."

In the subsequent weeks, Brian taught us how to throw clay, which is way harder than it sounds, as it involves throwing a ball of clay onto a spinning wheel and centring and immobilizing it. I never understood why something so difficult would be given such a flippant name. Throw—a casual act requiring no skill.

The section at the back of the studio where the wheels were kept smelled like petrichor for the first half-hour. Then a wet metallic smell hung in the air for the rest of class. Brian gave awfully specific instructions, imposing. "Anchor your elbows on your thighs, sit close to the wheel, wet the clay and your hands. Right hand pushes down, left hand pushes forward." As I tried to remember all the steps, my wet blobs of clay would leave the wheel, spinning, and splash all over me, from my hair to my boots. Sometimes I got the taste of earth in my mouth.

All the other students, I learned, had taken pottery lessons before and were many levels more advanced than I was. Like in my marriage, I was always a few steps behind.

When I was barely able to throw, my classmates had questions about pulling. When I got to pulling, with Rahel's help, on the third week, they had questions about trimming or sanding. My small hands could only throw small balls of clay, which meant I could only make shot glasses or teacups for a toddler's playset. One time I got Brian to throw a bigger ball of clay for me so I could make an adult-sized mug, but then while pulling, my fingers wouldn't wrap around the clay properly and the mug looked like a disfigured cat.

But Rahel was proud of me and all my disfigured pieces. She invited me to her fundraisers and dinner parties, always making sure I had someone to talk to. I was terrified of being alone with myself, with all the thoughts in my head that reminded me of the ways in which I had failed. It occurred to me one day as I stood at an intersection, paralyzed with fear, unable to decide whether I should turn left or go straight, that what I was most afraid of were the mean things I would tell myself later. For making a mistake, taking the wrong turn, being late, simply being inadequate. My parents had taught me to be true to my word, to be kind to others, to make wise decisions, but they had never taught me to be kind to myself. It was as if such a thing were a luxury back home, where fortunes could turn quickly.

In pottery class, the rest of the students began applying finishing touches: trimming, sanding, glazing. One woman was making a chessboard, chess pieces and all. I praised her for it, though I hated her guts. She ignored me.

So I took my small balls of clay and got to work. I used techniques I had seen on YouTube and started throwing. I gave up hope of making anything grand and focused on the clay, letting it give itself shape. I would start making a coffee mug, but the clay would want to be a bowl, and I would let it. By the final week, I had four shot glasses, an espresso cup, a couple of ice-cream bowls, and a candle holder.

Rahel said, "Look at you, taking your broken heart and making it into art."

One of my bestsellers is a cheese tray, hand-moulded and lumpy, glazed with red and white polka dots, with the words "FUCK YOU" painted on it. The description reads:

CeramicsByNilofer: Dinner Party
We invited friends over for a dinner party because I had heard that dinner parties are known to save marriages. I bought a fancy cheese plate for the occasion and bottles of wine, even though neither of us drank alcohol. My husband was his usual charming self, but halfway into the party one of the guests made a joke about people in sales being phonies.

The evening went downhill from there. My husband started talking very loudly and harassing the guest. I tried to calm him down, but he kept raising his voice. I passed him the cheese tray, hoping to distract him, but he knocked it out of my hand and screamed, "FUCK YOU!" in my face.

I designed this piece in memory of that day and how far I've come.

Do you want to turn the FUCK YOUS in your life into something beautiful? To order, go to my website.

• • •

One morning not long after the pottery class ended, I noticed that a haze was coming in through the small basement window, lighting up my finished pieces, which stood in a row. I could hear the kids' giggles and fast feet upstairs. I sat down in front of my little ceramics—hideous shot glasses, cups with cracks in them, bowls with uneven lips--and felt an incredible love for them. They were all the children I hadn't had, flawed and ugly, like me. In that moment, I felt happy. I took out my phone and snapped a picture of myself with my creations.

Three hours later, a helicopter flew me away from the highway. I had been on my way to visit our old home, overcome by emotion. I don't remember much of what happened on the road, but later, in the hospital room, I saw footage on the news. "At least one person is dead and several are critically injured in a multi-vehicle crash, stalling traffic eastbound on the 401 for hours," the reporter said.

A piece of metal had gone down my spine. I believe that I died that day, and the doctors and nurses brought me back to life. So I could start over.

Rahel took me in. When I was bedridden, with no agency over my limbs, everything that was causing me pain, all the regret about the past and wasted time and youth, all of that disappeared. In its place came a desperate hopelessness, a feeling that I couldn't breathe because I couldn't walk. As if without one, the other couldn't happen.

One day, staring at the popcorn ceiling in Rahel's house, the thought came to me that I could kill myself anytime I wanted. It would be hard without the use of my legs, but it could be done. Oddly, that thought gave me hope—I had a way out if I wanted. It gave me the freedom to think about other possibilities.

I began to take the physical therapy seriously. I had nothing to lose anymore, not even myself. For the first time in a long time, I was consumed by a brutal will to experience everything there is to experience. To get on my feet, to build something. In less than a year, I was walking again.

Soon, I learned other pottery techniques, like hand-building and slip-casting, which took some of the pressure off my small hands. When I first started making my pieces, I used to write in my journal about every item I made. Rahel was the one who suggested I sell them online, using the journal entries for context. She introduced me to her friend Kala, who sold peacock accessories online. Kala was gregarious. Somehow, she could get anyone besotted by the idea of wearing handmade jewellery. She showed me how to set up an online store and how to market my ceramics to people who have no idea what they want until they see it.

This one sells surprisingly well: a plain white coffee mug with the words "SIGN HERE" written in a legal-red glaze with an arrow underneath. The accompanying description reads:

CeramicsByNilofer: Sign Here
While recovering from a near-fatal car crush, I was also being harassed in court by my ex-husband over an uneven split of our joint assets. I was disabled, unemployed, and had no real-world skills.

I wrote my ex a heartfelt letter asking him to reconsider, as I did not have the resources to start from scratch. I reminded him of all the good times we had, building a life together in this country, all by ourselves.

His response was a letter from his lawyer stating his terms of separation and a bright yellow SIGN HERE *Post-it note.*

On a whim, with the little money I got from the divorce, I purchased a potter's wheel and a kiln and paid a deposit for the rent of a small studio in a strip mall. I began throwing and pulling and glazing, learning bit by bit. I put all my energy into the studio and my work. Piece by piece, making pottery has helped me put my body and my life back together.

I made this piece after I got the final paperwork from my ex-husband's lawyer.

Would you like one, as a sign of good things to come? To order, go to my website.

My workshop is a small room at the back of a yoga studio. The walls are painted white, and shelves line the sides of the L-shaped unit. I get to work early, when the man who sleeps in the entryway is still curled up over the vent and the storefront is soaked in sunlight. My ceramics catch the light, like hundreds of ugly little eager children who will love you no matter what.

This last one speaks to anyone who left their perfectly fine career because of something audacious, like wanting to be happy: a figurine of a doctor wearing teal scrubs and small round glasses, sitting in front of a potter's wheel.

CeramicsByNilofer: Doctor-Turned-Potter!
I come from a conservative Indian family in Hyderabad. I had finished five years of med school when a proposal for an arranged marriage came. My fiancé agreed that I could continue my education in Canada, but after we were married he changed his mind, and I couldn't afford to pay for it. Ten years later, I was divorced and left with next to nothing.

I turned a hobby into a business and started selling handmade ceramics. My parents back home cannot make sense of what I do. My father is a retired scientist and my mother is his devoted wife. Two of my four sisters are doctors, one is an engineer, and one has three kids. They all feel shame around our relatives, who refer to me as the doctor who turned into a potter. My parents and sisters have stopped going to family events because of me, the daughter and sister who could keep neither a husband nor a career.

I now have one full-time employee and three part-time employees to help with my business. I love what I do. I made this piece for all the people in the world who don't want to live someone else's dreams.

Do you want something to remind you to live your own dream? To order, go to my website.

Every now and then, I drive by my old neighbourhood with the big stone-faced homes on small lots. I park outside our old house with the red door and vaulted ceilings. I remember the time when I couldn't imagine a life beyond this house. I watch the latest occupants mowing the lawn or gardening and think how fortunate it is when life takes everything away from you so you can begin again. I let all the feelings in the world—the shame, the grief, the help-lessness, the confusion, the joy, the rage—come to me, and I hold them all, at least for a while.

Acknowledgements

MY PARENTS HAVE HAD to begin again many times. The first time, they moved to a small town in Saudi Arabia that no one had heard of, leaving behind everyone and everything they knew in India. They built a beautiful life, but it required much creativity and courage, and a good amount of delusion. My mother is one of the best storytellers I know—she can, to this day, relay a five-minute mundane incident in thirty minutes, adding internal monologues and character conflict. And my father is the finest artist in our family—he taught me how to make something beautiful out of nothing. Because of the two of them, I have the courage to write.

Virginia Woolf had a deeply hidden and inarticulate desire for something beyond the daily life. I am grateful to all those who love me who share this desire with me.

All my love to my Ahana, who can spin haikus and hilarities out of thin air. I strive to be as effortless, as joyful, and as funny as she is.

And Rumi. Although she has been utterly useless in the writing of this book, she came into my life exactly when I needed her.

Thank you to Karun for understanding what this book means to me, and for quietly supporting me. Shilpa, for being as restless and as loud as me, and for being the keeper of decades' worth of inside jokes. Soumya, for her love and prayers. Sheena, Supriya, Rachelle, for the sisterhood. Akshu, Abishek, Ekta, Sid, for their loving company and cheer. Katy, Ramsha, Abbie, for their professionalism and friendship. Dr. Reen, for worrying about my health so I could worry about the characters in this book.

Gratitude to my mentors and colleagues at Accenture, especially Jen Jackson and Ari Rowland, for showing me how to lead with courage and grace, and for believing in me.

A book doesn't happen in isolation. I am grateful to my teachers and friends at the University of Guelph and the University of Toronto scs for inspiring and supporting me. Michael Winter, Carrianne Leung, Catherine Bush, in whose classes many of these stories found their beginnings. Pasha Malla, Hoa Nguyen, Ayelet Tsabari, Shaughnessy Bishop Stall, Marina Nemat, Ranjini George, Lee Gowan, for their pedagogy.

Dionne Brand, for teaching me that when it comes to words, one cannot be ambivalent. Danila Botha, for giving me validation when I needed it the most, and for convincing me that my writing was good when no one else had read it.

Jamaluddin Aram, Evren Sezgin, Marjory Faion, for their friendship and their feedback, and for being co-dreamers in this journey. Sahar Golshan, Derek Mascarenhas, Anna Lee-Popham, Anna van Straubenzee, Nadia Shahbaz, Helen Kennedy, Alison Schofield, Kathy Belicki, for their loving support.

PEN Canada, Brendan de Caires, and the jury of the 2021 New Voices Award, Donna B. Nurse, Thea Lim, and Kaie Kellough, for recognizing the title story of this book the way they did. That was no small deal for me.

Huge gratitude to Canada Council for the Arts for its generous financial support.

The *Bristol Short Story Prize Anthology*, *Room* magazine, *Event* magazine, *Arc Poetry Magazine*, the *Quarantine Review*, and *The Unpublished City, Volume II*, for publishing my work and interviews. The *Malahat Review* for first publishing "Cake" and the *New Quarterly* for first publishing "Singing for the Gods."

Big gratitude to the characters in these stories for revealing themselves to me. As Arundhati Roy says, "Stories cull writers from the world."

Thank you to my agents at Transatlantic, Marilyn Biderman and Chelene Knight, for their trust in these stories. Gratitude to Sam Haywood, Cody Caetano, and Amanda Orozco for their kindness and cheer.

Immense gratitude to the team at House of Anansi Press, especially my extraordinary editor, Shirarose Wilensky, for her grace, expertise, and generosity, and for lifting this book and the wily women in it.

And finally, my biggest, deepest gratitude to Souvankham Thammavongsa. I am forever grateful for her brilliance. She gives me the courage to write the way I want to write. She is inimitable not just in her art but in life.

© Erna Suvajac

DEEPA RAJAGOPALAN won the 2021 RBC/PEN Canada New Voices Award. Her work has appeared in literary magazines and anthologies such as the *Bristol Short Story Prize Anthology*, the *New Quarterly*, *Room*, the *Malahat Review*, *Event*, and *Arc Poetry Magazine*. She has an MFA in creative writing from the University of Guelph. Born to Indian parents in Saudi Arabia, she has lived in many cities across India, the US, and Canada.